Hooky
VOLUME 3

MÍRIAM BONASTRE TUR

CLARION BOOKS
IMPRINTS OF HARPERCOLLINSPUBLISHERS

HARPER
alley

CLARION BOOKS IS AN IMPRINT OF HARPERCOLLINS PUBLISHERS.
HARPERALLEY IS AN IMPRINT OF HARPERCOLLINS PUBLISHERS.

HOOKY VOLUME 3

ISBN 978-0-35-869358-1 — ISBN 978-0-35-869357-4 (PBK.)
ISBN 978-0-06-334183-8 (SIGNED EDITION)

LETTERING BY NATALIE FONDRIEST

PB: 23-WOZ-3
HC: 23-WOZ-2

FIRST EDITION
A DIGITAL VERSION OF HOOKY WAS ORIGINALLY PUBLISHED ON
WEBTOON IN 2015.

4

6

NICO...

HERE, DANI.

TRY THIS, IT MIGHT TRIGGER SOME MEMORIES.

...

DANI...

PLEASE...

JUST A BITE!

YOUR MAJESTY?

MARK SAID YOU USED TO ENJOY IT.

...WHO?

...YOU SERIOUSLY DON'T REMEMBER?

...

I DON'T KNOW WHAT ELSE TO DO...

I'VE ASKED MYSELF IF YOU COULD HEAR ME FOR QUITE SOME TIME--

EVEN IF I'M BY YOUR SIDE, EVEN IF I SCREAM, I'M NOT EVEN SURE IF MY VOICE ACTUALLY REACHES YOU.

11

IT MEANS THAT I'LL DO EVERYTHING I CAN TO MAKE YOU FEEL MORE LIKE YOUR OLD SELF.

GET OUT OF MY SIGHT.

BUT DANI, WHAT...?

DON'T CALL ME DANI. I'M YOUR QUEEN.

LISTEN, GIRL...

DON'T GET RID OF HIM YET.

WHY?

HE COULD BE USEFUL TO US IN THE FUTURE.

EVEN IF IT PAINS YOU TO ADMIT THAT, BECAUSE I KNOW YOU ONLY WISH TO SEE ALL WITCHES FALL,

TO SEE OUR KIND MARGINALIZED AND MURDERED. I WON'T ALLOW IT.

MOREOVER, YOUR DESPAIR IS DELICIOUS.

...SEE YOU SOON.

12

I'VE BEEN WORKING ON THIS SINCE WE GOT HERE, THREE YEARS AGO.

I COULDN'T STAND THE IDEA OF BEING LOCKED INSIDE THE CASTLE, EVEN IF IT WAS FOR MY OWN SAFETY, WHILE OUTSIDE THE BATTLE WAS RAGING.

I WANTED TO GET OUT AND FIGHT, BUT I REALIZED I COULDN'T JUST GO THERE EMPTY-HANDED.

I NEEDED A PLAN.

I NEEDED TO BECOME STRONGER.

AND SO, I TRIED TO FIND INFORMATION ABOUT MAGIC.

IT WAS HARD, SINCE YOUR FATHER FORBADE ANYTHING RELATED TO WITCHCRAFT YEARS AGO.

BUT THANKS TO MY PERSUASIVE SKILLS, I GOT SOME PEOPLE TO BRING ME BOOKS FROM OTHER LOCATIONS.

I THOUGHT YOU DIDN'T WANT TO MARRY ME!

CALM DOWN, MONICA.

YOU HAVE TO DO THIS.

HE'S NOT COMING BACK ANYWAY.

THUMP THUMP

HE LEFT.

SINCE THEN, THINGS HAVE GOTTEN WORSE.

HE SAID HE'D BE BACK SOON.

THERE WAS A BIG FIGHT BETWEEN THE SORCERERS AND KING EDGAR'S SOLDIERS.

THAT WAS THE LAST TIME I SAW DORIAN.

MANY DIED, BUT DANI AND HER MOTHER FLED BEFORE I COULD SEE HER AND TELL HER WHAT HAD REALLY HAPPENED.

19

LATER, THEY EXPLAINED THE PLAN TO ME.

DORIAN WAS GOING TO MEET MARK AND AISHA FAR AWAY, IN A SAFE PLACE.

THE FIRST PART OF THE PLAN WORKED.

KING EDGAR AND EVERYONE ELSE THOUGHT DORIAN WAS DEAD.

BUT THE SECOND PART, MEETING HIM, NEVER HAPPENED.

MARK AND AISHA LOOKED FOR HIM AROUND THE MEETING POINT FOR WEEKS.

BUT DORIAN NEVER SHOWED UP.

MEANWHILE, I WAS TRAPPED IN MY OWN PERSONAL HELL.

I HAD LOST MY ENTIRE FAMILY.

AND I WAS LIVING UNDER THE WATCHFUL EYE OF WILLIAM'S FATHER.

WHO ONLY HOPED THAT I WOULD MARRY HIS SON TO UNITE THE KINGDOMS.

AND THUS HAVE THE POWER TO FINALLY DESTROY THE WITCHES.

NICO SNEAKED OUT AS OFTEN AS HE COULD

GIVING US UPDATES ABOUT DANI AND ASKING FOR HELP.

BUT WE COULDN'T GET CLOSE TO HER.

EVERY TIME THE KING SENT A MESSENGER OR A SPY, THEY ENDED UP BURNED AT THE GATES OF THE CITY.

AT A CERTAIN POINT, I DECIDED TO ACT.

I WANTED TO DO SOMETHING TO SAVE DANI.

I RESEARCHED, PRACTICED, AND BECAME STRONGER.

MARRYING WILLIAM IS ESSENTIAL TO SECURE THE SUPPORT OF THE NOBILITY AND THE PEOPLE

AND TO OBTAIN THE FULL STRENGTH OF THE ARMIES OF BOTH KINGDOMS.

THE PROMISE OF LOVE I MADE TO DORIAN

HAS FALLEN SO FAR BEHIND ME IN TIME THAT IT NOW SEEMS LIKE CHILD'S PLAY.

IT HAS BEEN THREE YEARS SINCE HE LEFT

AND MY MEMORIES OF THAT TIME HAVE SLOWLY FADED.

AFTER ALL, I ONLY SPENT ONE YEAR OF MY LIFE WITH DORIAN.

I DON'T EVEN KNOW ANYMORE WHAT PART OF HIM IS REAL...

...AND WHAT PART IS JUST AN IDEALIZED MEMORY.

EVEN THOUGH...

SOMETIMES I STILL DREAM ABOUT HIM

ABOUT TALKING AND LAUGHING TOGETHER

AND WHEN I WAKE UP, I FEEL VERY LONELY.

MONICA?

I THOUGHT YOU DIDN'T WANT TO MARRY ME!

YOU SAID NO EVERY SINGLE TIME MY FATHER MENTIONED IT!

IF I HAD MARRIED YOU, YOUR FATHER WOULD'VE USED THAT AS AN EXCUSE TO CLAIM MY FATHER'S KINGDOM!

HE WOULD'VE ENTERED IT WITH HIS ARMY TO KILL ALL THE WITCHES!

HE WOULD'VE HARMED DANI AS WELL AS OTHER INNOCENTS.

I WILL DEFEAT THE QUEEN, DANI, BUT I WANNA DO IT MY OWN WAY.

DO YOU THINK YOU CAN HEAL HER?

I HOPE SO.

THIS HAS BEEN THE MAIN FOCUS OF MY STUDIES. AN ANTIDOTE FOR DANI.

I KNOW.

OH NO, IT BROKE!

YOU NEED TO BE VERY GENTLE WHEN YOU REMOVE THE MOLD!

IF YOU'RE NOT PATIENT, YOU'LL NEVER BE ABLE TO MAKE ONE OF OUR FAMOUS EVANS-CAFÉ-STYLE APPLE PIES!

BUT IT CAN STILL BE EATEN, RIGHT?!

I DON'T THINK PEOPLE WILL MIND IF IT'S A BIT CRUMBLED...!

AH!

PENDRAGON, MY OLD FRIEND!

HELLO, EVANS.

I'M SORRY I VANISHED LIKE THAT... I KNOW YOU ALL NEEDED ME...

THE ONLY THING THAT MATTERS IS THAT YOU'RE OK. WE THOUGHT YOU WERE DEAD!

I DIDN'T COME BACK FOR PLEASURE, THERE'S STILL SOMETHING I NEED TO DO...

I CAN'T HIDE THIS ANYMORE...

CARLO'S JOURNEY

3 YEARS AGO

HOW CHILLY...

MARK, WE SHOULD GO BACK.

WE'VE BEEN OUTSIDE FOR TOO LONG, THERE'S NO TRACE OF DORIAN...

NO! WE CAN'T JUST LEAVE HIM!

WHY ISN'T HE HERE?! WHAT IF SOMETHING HAPPENED TO HIM?! WHAT IF HE NEEDS OUR HELP...?!

DO YOU THINK HE'S...? UH...

BUT THIS IS SO FRUSTRATING!

WE'LL FIND HIM!

BUT FIRST, WE NEED TO GO BACK. WE'RE ALMOST OUT OF FOOD AND WE DON'T HAVE ANY LEADS.

EH, MARK, LISTEN, I DON'T...!

I'M SORRY, I DIDN'T MEAN THAT!

I KNOW.

28

WHO KNOWS, PERHAPS HE HAS ALREADY RESCUED DANI AND THEY'RE BOTH SAFE, AT HOME.

DO YOU THINK SO...?

I DON'T KNOW.

BUT WE NEED TO LEAVE.

...ALL RIGHT THEN.

COME ON, CARLO, LET'S GET GOING!

WE SHOULD PROBABLY GO TO THE CAFÉ...

OH! WILL I MEET YOUR FATHER THEN?

DOES HE LOOK LIKE YOU, MARK?

HE'S MORE MUSCULAR, BUT YE....

AAAARGH!!

LET GO, CARLO!

WHAT IS GOING ON WITH YOU?!

LET GOOO!

...

31

AH, I THINK I CAN HELP WITH THAT.

EH?

I'LL DEFEAT THAT DRAGON!

IT'S NOT THE FIRST TIME I FACED ONE!

I'M COMING WITH YOU! WE'LL BEAT IT UP!

NO, WAIT.

AISHA.

NOT A CHANCE!

HOLD IT THERE!

POW

ARGH!

UGH...

ALL RIGHT, DAMIEN...

YOU'RE REALLY DUMB, MARK.

NOBODY NEEDS TO DIRECTLY FACE THE DRAGON.

WE'LL USE THE DUMMY AS A BAIT. AS SOON AS IT GETS DISTRACTED, WE'LL GIVE DORIAN THE ANTIDOTE!

IN ORDER TO GET THE ANTIDOTE, WE MUST FIGURE OUT THE TYPE OF VENOM...

ISN'T THAT RIGHT, PENDRAGON?

... HE'S DEAD, GUYS.

I'M SORRY, BUT YOU MUST ACCEPT THAT.

DID YOU FIND ANYTHING, DAMIEN?

I'M LOOKING THROUGH MONICA'S STUDIES ON POTIONS.

THEY ARE VERY THOROUGH,

BUT I CAN'T FIND ANY ANTIDOTE TO THE POISON MASTER PENDRAGON GAVE DORIAN.

SO, I CHOSE A GENERAL HEALING POTION.

BUT, MONICA HIGHLIGHTED THIS PARTICULAR RECIPE.

SHE EVEN ADDED A LOT OF EXCLAMATION MARKS AND LITTLE STARS.

IT'S USED TO HEAL MINOR SPELLS, DIFFERENT TYPES OF WOUNDS...

HOW'S IT GOING?

DON'T MAKE HIM NERVOUS, IT'S A DELICATE MOMENT.

WHOA!

BOOM

AH, OF COURSE!

I KNOW THAT POTION!

I REMEMBER WHEN THEY MADE IT FOR THE FIRST TIME!

I'M SO GLAD TO SEE YOU!

WHAT ARE YOU ALL DOING HERE? YOU LOOK WEIRD...

WHAT THE HELL ARE YOU SAYING, YOU'RE THE ONE LOOKING WEIRD HERE!!

YOU LOOK HORRIBLE!!

NICO, CALM DOWN...

ALTHOUGH HE DOES INDEED LOOK DREADFUL.

IT'S SO CREEPY, YOU LOOK LIKE A CORPSE!!

INCREDIBLE... I DIDN'T THINK WE'D FIND HIM...

WHAT ARE YOU TALKING ABOUT!

YOU'VE NEVER LOST HOPE, MARK!

EVEN THOUGH, "ALIVE"...

I DON'T REALLY KNOW IF HE'S THAT ALIVE...

UH...

UGH...

DORIAN!!

AH!

49

MAGIC? THAT'S HOW CURSES WORK.

PRINCE WILLIAM WAS ALSO IN A DEEP SLUMBER FOR MONTHS AND HE DIDN'T STARVE TO DEATH.

RIGHT, BUT DORIAN GREW UP...

LOOK AT HIM, HE'S TALLER, HE GOT BIGGER. HE MUST HAVE EATEN SOMETHING.

DO YOU WANT ME TO CARRY DORIAN FOR A BIT, MARK?

NO, DON'T WORRY, HE WEIGHS PRACTICALLY NOTHING.

YES, HE'S SO THIN... YOU CAN CLEARLY SEE HE HASN'T EATEN IN YEARS.

HOW CAN HE POSSIBLY BE ALIVE, THEN?

I BET THE DRAGON WAS TAKING CARE OF HIM. GIVING HIM REGURGITATED FOOD!

JUST LIKE MOTHER BIRDS WHEN THEY FEED THEIR BABIES!

AISHA...

NO... IT WAS MAGIC, WASN'T IT?

YUCK...

OH, WOW.

THE BRIDGE COLLAPSED.

EH!

HEY!

NO, ABSOLUTELY NOT!

DON'T YOU DARE BURY A CORPSE UNDER THIS BRIDGE!

IF YOU MESSED UP, DEAL WITH IT ON YOUR OWN, WE'RE WORKING HERE!

WE DIDN'T KILL ANYONE!

THAT'S MY BROTHER, WHO JUST FAINTED...

YEAH, THAT'S RIGHT.

SO DO YOU KNOW OF ANY SAFE PLACE WHERE WE COULD SLEEP OR EAT SOMETHING?

YOU CAME ACROSS THE RIGHT PERSON!

I'VE LIVED HERE MY ENTIRE LIFE, SINCE I WAS A LITTLE BOY!

THIS PLACE USED TO BE A FIELD BACK THEN!

...

EHM... IT'S STILL A FIELD.

I KNOW! AND IT'S ALL BECAUSE OF THIS STUPID WAR BETWEEN WITCHES AND ANTI-WITCHCRAFT PEOPLE!

WITHOUT THEIR NONSENSE, WE WOULD BE SUCH A PROSPEROUS COUNTRY!

AND THESE FIELDS WOULD BE FULL OF SCHOOLS, HOSPITALS, LIBRARIES AND MANY, MANY PUBS!

IF ONLY THEY'D LET ME LEARN MAGIC, I'D PUT EVERYONE RIGHT BACK INTO LINE!

YOU! STOP CHATTERING AND GET BACK TO WORK!

THE BRIDGE WON'T BUILD ITSELF!!

SLAP

AND YOU, GUYS, IF YOU'RE LOOKING FOR A PLACE TO STAY, JUST GO SOUTH.

YOU'LL BE AT THE VILLAGE IN THREE HOURS.

THANKS A LOT, SIR!

GOOD LUCK!

EH... DID YOU NOTICE?

THOSE DUDES... THOSE DUDES WEREN'T WITCHES, OF COURSE. BUT THEY DIDN'T SEEM AFRAID OF MAGIC.

AH, THAT'S TRUE!

YES, I'VE ALSO NOTICED THAT! HOW COOL!

YEAH, IT'S...

IT'S WEIRD.

BESIDES, THIS VILLAGE WAS PROBABLY TAKEN BY DANI'S ARMY... MANY PEOPLE LIVE ON THE STREET,

HALF OF THE BUILDINGS WERE BURNT DOWN.

THEY'VE BEEN THROUGH QUITE A LOT, AND THEY SEEM AFRAID OF THE QUEEN AND HER PEOPLE, YET...

...

EH, THEY SAID THERE ARE VACANT ROOMS!

AWESOME! WE'RE LUCKY!

TOMORROW WE'LL HAVE TO DEAL WITH A COMPLICATED MISSION.

AND WHAT IS THAT...?

TELLING DORIAN WHAT HAPPENED.

MAKING HIM UNDERSTAND THAT HE'S BEEN ASLEEP FOR THREE YEARS.

DO YOU THINK HE'LL TAKE IT WELL? OR WILL HE GO CRAZY?

YES, HE'LL MANAGE.

I'M SURE HE'LL HELP US ALL WITH DANI.

SO... ARE YOU HUNGRY?

DO YOU WANNA GO DOWN AND EAT SOMETHING?

YEAH, I'M STARVING.

WHAT ARE WE GONNA DO WITH THIS ONE, THEN?

YEAH... WE CAN'T GO DOWN WITH THE MASTER TIED UP LIKE A CRIMINAL...

WE'RE WALKING AROUND WITH AN OLD MAN TIED UP AND SOME KIND OF PASSED-OUT ZOMBIE ON OUR BACKS.

I'M ACTUALLY SURPRISED THEY DIDN'T CALL THE GUARDS!

BUT WE CAN'T RISK UNTYING HIM. WE NEED TO KEEP AN EYE ON HIM FOR NOW.

TOMORROW MORNING WE'LL HEAD TO MONICA'S CASTLE, AND WE'LL LOCK HIM UP IN THE DUNGEON.

HEY, DON'T TALK AS IF I'M NOT EVEN HERE...

SINCE WE WILL BE TAKING PENDRAGON TO THE DUNGEON, IT LOOKS LIKE WE WILL ACTUALLY BE ABLE TO ATTEND WILLIAM AND MONICA'S WEDDING.

OH, THAT'S COOL!

MY BROTHER AND MOTHER WILL DEFINITELY BE THERE!

HERE'S WHAT YOU'VE ASKED FOR.

THANKS!

OH, AND JUST A QUESTION...

ARE YOU WITCHES, BY ANY CHANCE?

DORIAN DISAPPEARED!! HE'S NOT HERE!!

ARE YOU KIDDING ME?!

OH, HE WAS KIDNAPPED!

WHERE IS THAT IDIOT?!

MMH?

OH...?

AH, GUYS, YOU FINALLY WOKE UP!

WELL, YOU WERE REALLY STARVING.

YOU'RE LOOKING BETTER NOW!

I NEED TO GO. THANK YOU FOR EVERYTHING!

EH, YOU'VE GOT TO PAY FOR THE FOOD, KID!

I DON'T HAVE ANY MONEY ON ME.

BUT MY FRIENDS ARE SLEEPING UPSTAIRS! THEY'LL PAY.

WILL YOU COME BACK...?

YES.

BUT BEFORE THAT, THERE'S SOMETHING IMPORTANT I NEED TO DO...

PAQUITA HAIRDRESSER

ARE YOU SURE YOU WANNA CUT IT?

I'M SURE, CUT IT.

DON'T DO IT. IT'S SUCH A SHAME!

LONG HAIR SUITS YOU WELL...

I CAN'T GO OUT LIKE THIS; I LOOK LIKE A CRIMINAL.

MY FATHER WOULD FREAK OUT...

ALL RIGHT THEN...

PERFECT, I LOOK SO MUCH BETTER!

NOW I CAN RECOGNIZE MYSELF!

EVEN THOUGH SOMETHING IS STILL OFF...

EH... EXCUSE ME... HOW OLD DO I LOOK?

WELL, I DON'T KNOW... SIXTEEN? SEVENTEEN?

SIXTEEN?!

THAT MEANS I SLEPT FOR THREE YEARS??

IS SHE ALIVE...?

AGH... I NEED TO KNOW...

BUT I CAN'T JUST ASK... I DON'T KNOW ABOUT THE CURRENT SITUATION.

I DON'T EVEN KNOW WHAT YEAR IT IS OR WHERE I AM. IT COULD BE DANGEROUS.

I'LL JUST GO WAKE UP NICO AND THE OTHERS... OR...

I HAVE AN IDEA.

DO YOU HAVE A NEWSPAPER BY ANY CHANCE?

WHAT?

A NEWSPAPER?

...

... NO.

THERE'S NO SUCH THING HERE, I DON'T KNOW WHERE YOU GOT THAT INFORMATION.

PLEASE LEAVE.

WHA...?

IT'S FIVE FOR THE HAIRCUT.

AH... I DON'T HAVE ANY MONEY ON ME...

WHAT?!

DID YOU THINK WE'D WORK FOR FREE BECAUSE OF YOUR PRETTY FACE?!

PAY US!!

UHM...

I CAN FIX YOUR WINDOW, IF YOU WANT.

BUT YOU'LL NEED TO LEAVE ME ALONE FOR A SECOND.

I PROMISE I WON'T RUN AWAY. BUT PLEASE, DON'T COME BACK UNTIL I TELL YOU TO DO SO.

... SERIOUSLY, THIS GUY...?

I LOCKED THE DOOR. LET HIM TRY ANYTHING HE WANTS.

OOOOH...

INCREDIBLE...

WELL, I HOPE THIS WORKS AS A PAYMENT!

THANK YOU SO MUCH FOR EVERYTHING!

HE'S A WITCH.

DOES HE THINK WE'RE STUPID??

...

FOLLOW ME, BOY...

AH!

EH?

REALLY?

HERE HE IS...

THE YOUNG MAN WHO HAS BEEN CAUSING TROUBLE IN THE VILLAGE ALL MORNING...

SO YOU'RE LOOKING FOR A NEWSPAPER, MMMH?

LONG TIME NO SEE, DORIAN...

AH?! IT'S YOU!

WHO WAS IT?!

WHO WAS HIDING IN THE SWAMP?!

TELL US ALREADY, DORIAN!

YOU DON'T NEED TO RECOUNT YOUR MORNING IN FULL DETAIL!

EH? IT'S QUITE IMPORTANT.

IN THE END, IT TURNED OUT EVERYONE WAS TRYING TO HELP ME, EVEN IF I COULDN'T SEE THAT.

LOOK, I FOUND THE NEWSPAPER.

HMMM...? THIS NEWSPAPER IS...?

ARE THERE ANY ARTICLES ABOUT WITCHCRAFT?

"WEEKLY RECIPE: THIS POTION WILL MAKE YOUR POTATOES GROW IN JUST A FEW HOURS."

WHAT IS THIS...?

THE INSURGENT WITCH

AH! TAKE A LOOK AT THE COVER, MARK...!!

THE INSURGENT WITCH

WHAT'S THIS DRAWING RIGHT HERE...?

IT'S ALEX!!

WHAT'S THIS ALL ABOUT?!

... OH!

HEY!

HI MARK! NICO! LONG TIME NO SEE.

YOU BOTH GREW UP SO FAST!

NOAH! BARRY! WHAT ARE YOU DOING HERE?!

DO YOU LIKE OUR SECRET NEWSPAPER?

GENT WITCH

BUT... WHAT IS IT?

IT'S AN ILLEGAL PUBLICATION.

WE THINK THAT THE WITCH'S REIGN IS ONLY ADDING MORE TROUBLE TO THE CONFLICT.

AND WE WANTED TO OFFER A DIFFERENT PERSPECTIVE,

TO SHOW THAT WITCHES DON'T AGREE WITH THE WYTTES' POLICIES.

WELL... MOST OF THE WYTTES.

SORRY, DORIAN.

IT'S OK.

WE PUBLISHED IT FOR THE PEOPLE. ALL OF THE PEOPLE.

WE'RE TRYING TO KEEP IT A SECRET SINCE WE'D END UP AT THE STAKE IF DANI'S ARMY CATCHES US.

I KNOW I WAS ASLEEP FOR THREE YEARS, FOR SOME REASON.

AND I KNOW THAT DURING THIS TIME, DANI HAS BECOME EVIL.

BUT I DON'T BELIEVE IT.

IT ALL HAS TO DO WITH MY MOTHER.

AND I WILL GO RESCUE HER TODAY.

THEY SAID SHE'S A COLD, CRUEL QUEEN AND THAT SHE DID HORRIBLE THINGS, SHE KILLED PEOPLE.

DORIAN...!

YOU'RE RIGHT, DORIAN. DANI ISN'T EVIL.

BUT SHE IS COLD.

IT'S ALMOST AS IF...

AS IF SHE WERE NOT HERSELF ANYMORE...

SHE HAS BEEN ABSENT SINCE THE MOMENT SHE THOUGHT YOU WERE DEAD.

SO IT'S MY FAULT...

I FAILED HER.

THREE YEARS... I CAN'T BELIEVE IT.

I PROMISED I WOULD GET HER OUT OF THERE AND IT TOOK ME THREE YEARS...

IT'S NOT YOUR FAULT, DORIAN!

NO! IT'S...

IT'S THE MASTER'S FAULT.

BUT NOW THAT YOU'RE HERE, EVERYTHING WILL BE FINE!

I KNOW YOU'RE THE ONLY ONE WHO CAN MAKE DANI COME BACK TO HER SENSES!

SHE'LL GO BACK TO NORMAL AS SOON AS SHE SEES YOU!

YES... I THINK SO TOO.

ALL IS NOT LOST, IT SEEMS...

NOT EVERYONE HATES WITCHES...

ACTUALLY, IT'S PRETTY WEIRD BUT PEOPLE SEEM TO BE A LOT LESS FRIGHTENED NOW!

THAT'S BECAUSE PEOPLE ONLY WANT TO LIVE IN PEACE.

THAT'S SOMETHING WE HAVE IN COMMON.

AND MAGIC IS REALLY CONVENIENT!

MY POTATOES GREW IN JUST 3 HOURS!

AND NOW A HERO HAS ARRIVED!

A HERO?! NO, I AM NOT...!

WE'VE ALSO GOT MONICA'S PLAN.

I'M SURE ONE OF THEM WILL BRING DANI BACK.

IF DORIAN'S THE "HERO", MONICA'S GONNA GET MAD.

SHE ALWAYS SAID SHE WANTED A STATUE BUILT IN HER HONOR IN THE TOWN SQUARE.

AH! SPEAKING OF MONICA...

DORIAN, DO YOU KNOW...?

WELL...!

UM... DO YOU KNOW ANYTHING ABOUT MONICA OR NOT?

HAVE YOU FULLY READ THE NEWSPAPER...?

EH? NOT YET, I WAS DOING THAT WHEN YOU CAME DOWNSTAIRS.

WHY ARE YOU ASKING?

ROYAL WEDDIN

HUH?! WE... WELL... I KNOW SHE'S SAFE AND SOUND IN THE CASTLE OF WILLIAM'S FATHER!

IS THAT RIGHT?

UM... YES...

TRUTH IS, I'VE GIVEN THIS MATTER A LOT OF THOUGHT...

AND I'VE GOT A SERIOUS PROBLEM....

WHAT PROBLEM?

HOW OLD IS MONICA NOW?

EIGHTEEN, JUST LIKE ME.

SHE'S AN ADULT!

HOW AM I SUPPOSED TO TALK TO HER NOW?!

DON'T WORRY, SHE'S DYING TO SEE YOU.

PRECISELY! I'VE MADE HER WAIT THREE YEARS. IT'S ONLY BEEN A WHILE FOR ME.

I BET SHE'S FURIOUS!

I REMEMBER IT PERFECTLY. IT ONLY HAPPENED A FEW HOURS AGO...

SHE PROMISED SHE'D WAIT FOR ME...

IT LOOKED LIKE...

IT LOOKED LIKE WE WERE BOTH ON THE SAME PAGE...

BUT NOW...

WHAT IS SHE GONNA THINK WHEN SHE SEES ME?!

WHO'S THIS KID?!

DO YOU THINK I'M GONNA PLAY HIDE AND SEEK WITH YOU, DORIAN?

WHAT A FREAK...

SHE'LL THINK I'M RIDICULOUS!

I REALLY DON'T GET ALL THE FUSS...

WHAT DIFFERENCE DOES IT MAKE IF IT TOOK YOU A WHILE TO COME BACK?

WAIT, AISHA... IT'S JUST THAT DORIAN AND MONICA...

BESIDES, I'M SURE SHE HAS MORE IMPORTANT THINGS TO THINK ABOUT WITH THE WHOLE WEDDING THING.

HUH?

OH, MONICA, THOSE EARRINGS WILL LOOK WONDERFUL WITH YOUR WEDDING DRESS!

COME ON, ANNE! THEY LOOK TERRIBLE!

THESE ONES SUIT HER BETTER. THEY'RE MORE DELICATE AND ELEGANT.

LET MONICA DECIDE!

COME ON! WHICH ONE'S THE BEST?

THE ONES I CHOSE FOR YOU, RIGHT?

... MONICA, ANSWER!

I'M SORRY, GIRLS. I HAVE TO GO!!

HUH? WHERE ARE YOU GOING?!

YOU CAN'T GO OUT LIKE THIS! YOU'RE NAKED!

MMMH??

AH! DAMIEN?!

DAMIEN!!

ARE YOU ALREADY BACK?!

HI, MONICA.

AH...

THAT SMILE...

HOW DID IT GO?

WHERE ARE THE OTHERS?

MONICA... LISTEN.

WE FOUND DORIAN.

HE'S ALIVE AND WELL.

VERY STRONG AND DETERMINED TO SAVE DANI.

DORIAN...!

UH...

HERE, I'LL HELP YOU WITH THAT.

YOU SEEM QUITE LONELY.

AND YOU SEEM VERY HAPPY.

... OF COURSE.

WE FOUND DORIAN, SAFE AND SOUND.

AT THIS VERY MOMENT HE'S GOING TO RESCUE DANI. LOOKS PROMISING.

...IS THE WEDDING STILL THAT URGENT, THEN?

YES.

IF DORIAN DOESN'T SUCCEED, WE'VE GOT MONICA'S PLAN.

WE CAN'T SUDDENLY CALL OFF THE WEDDING, SPOILING THE WHOLE PLAN.

MOREOVER, SOONER OR LATER, YOU WOULD'VE ENDED UP MARRYING MONICA ANYWAYS, YOU'VE ALWAYS KNOWN THAT.

DOES IT BOTHER YOU?

MY WEDDING, I MEAN.

WHY WOULD IT BOTHER ME?

YOU SAID IT YOURSELF, NOTHING WILL CHANGE. WE'LL STILL BE FRIENDS AS USUAL.

BUT DAMIEN,

WHAT IS IT THAT YOU WANT?

WHAT DO YOU WANT, WILL?

WHAT DO I WANT...?

I NEED TO MARRY PRINCESS MONICA.

IT'S IMPORTANT TO THE KINGDOM.

THAT DOESN'T ANSWER MY QUESTION.

BONG BONG

BONG BONG

BONG

YET YOU'VE CHOSEN TO RESCUE DANI INSTEAD OF TRYING TO STOP THE WEDDING.

IT MAKES SENSE.

WHAT HAPPENED BETWEEN US TOOK PLACE A LONG TIME AGO...

IT WAS JUST CHILD'S PLAY...

AND NOW...

I'M ABOUT TO BECOME A MARRIED WOMAN.

I HAVE EVERYTHING PLANNED DOWN TO THE LAST DETAIL.

THE PERFECT DRESS.

THE IDEAL BANQUET.

THE PEOPLE ARE EUPHORIC.

HOW CAN YOU ALLOW THIS, DANI?

ARE YOU THERE?

WHAT HAVE THEY DONE TO YOU?

I HOPE MY PLAN WORKS...

RUN, GET OVER THERE!

REMEMBER THE REHEARSALS!

THEY'LL SEE!

YOU SAID IT'D BE A WONDERFUL WEDDING!

IF ONLY I HAD KNOWN, I'D HAVE SIGNED UP FOR YOUR MOTHER'S PICNIC!

IS EVERYONE READY?

YES! NOW, MR. DAMIEN!

THIS SPELL...!

DAMIEN!

THE RIGHT MOMENT, YOU SAID?

INDEED.

YOU GOT HERE JUST IN TIME FOR THE PARTY.

AH... DID IT WORK...?

UH...

UGH...

YUCK...

UH...

DANI...?

A... ARE YOU OK?

DANI...

DON'T TOUCH ME.

DANI?!

LET GO, YOU'RE HURTING ME!

I'M SORRY IF IT TASTED BAD, DON'T PUKE IT UP THOUGH!

AH... SHE GOT AWAY.

SHE DESTROYED THE CATHEDRAL... MONICA'S PLAN DIDN'T WORK, IN THE END...

...

WE'LL NEED TO MOVE ON TO PLAN B AND USE OUR JOINED ARMIES.

WE'LL HAVE WAY MORE SUPPORT NOW THAT WE'RE MARRIED.

THAT'S NOT TRUE...

MY PLAN ACTUALLY DID SOMETHING.

ISN'T THAT TRUE, MRS. WYTTE...?

CHAPTER 65

WE'RE ALMOST THERE! I CAN'T BELIEVE IT; I'LL FINALLY SEE DANI!

WOW... I REMEMBERED THIS PALACE WAY... BRIGHTER.

HAVE YOU BEEN HERE BEFORE?

OF COURSE! I'VE SPENT MANY SUMMERS HERE.

MY BROTHER AND I WOULD SPEND THE DAY PLAYING WITH MONICA, WILL, DAMIEN, IVY AND ANNE.

OH, I WAS ONLY HERE ONCE.

THE DAY OF THE GREAT BALL THE KING ORGANIZED IN HOPES OF REESTABLISHING PEACE DURING THE WAR AGAINST WITCHES...

IT DIDN'T GO WELL.

CLEARLY.

WHAT MATTERS THE MOST IS HOW MARK WAS DRESSED THAT DAY!

I'LL REMEMBER THOSE SILLY LITTLE PINK PANTS 'TIL THE DAY I DIE!

HA-HA!

105

BUT...

WHERE?

...

WILL...

CAN YOU JUST STOP STARING AT ME? YOU'RE GETTING ON MY NERVES. IF YOU DON'T STOP, I'LL KICK YOUR ASS.

THIS IS NOT ACCEPTABLE!

MONICA!!

...

YOU CAN'T KILL MRS. WYTTE!

SHE'S DAMIEN'S MUM! AND DORIAN'S AND DANIELA'S! IF YOU LOVE THEM, YOU CAN'T DO THIS!

WELL, IT'S NOT JUST MY CHOICE TO MAKE.

REMEMBER YOU ARE THE KING NOW.

WELL, THEN... I FORBID YOU!

WILLIAM... DROP IT.

THAT'S NOT HOW YOU FIX THINGS.

LOOK.

DON'T ASSUME I'VE SPENT YEARS STUDYING, RESEARCHING, AND IMPROVING...

... JUST TO MAKE A SLIGHTLY STRONGER HEALING POTION.

NO...

I'VE STILL GOT MANY ACES UP MY SLEEVE.

WHAT ARE YOU GONNA DO WITH THAT?

WHAT'S THAT POTION FOR?

MONICA!

...

TAKE IT.

YES, YOUR MAJESTY.

YOU ALREADY KNOW WHAT TO DO WITH IT.

BE DISCREET.

AT YOUR SERVICE, YOUR MAJESTY.

WE'RE HERE...

LAST TIME I WAS HERE FEELS LIKE YESTERDAY!

ONE SECOND, MARK, I NEED TO PUT THE LITTLE ONE IN MY BACKPACK!

HE COULD SCARE SOMEBODY IF THEY SEE HIM...

YOU SHOULD NAME HIM! GIVE HIM A POWERFUL NAME! LIKE BLOODY OR MONSTROUS...

COME ON, GET IN! BE GOOD. LOOK HOW CARLO'S HIDING!

YES, NICO TOO! I'M SURE THEY'D BE SCARED OF HIS FIERCENESS IF THEY SAW HIM...

THAT'S ENOUGH, IDIOT! I'D LIKE TO SEE YOU WITH MY SIZE!!

DEATH WING...

DEVIL...

BREATH OF HELL...

TORMENT OF HEAVENS...

I WOULDN'T BE AS CUTE AS YOU, THAT'S FOR SURE.

WOW... EVERYTHING'S BASICALLY THE SAME...

EVEN THOUGH IT'S CLEAR THAT DANI'S ARMY HASN'T CONQUERED THESE LANDS YET...

PEOPLE SEEM VERY QUIET.

UH...

IT WAS HERE...

THE PLACE WHERE THEY WERE GONNA KILL ME FOR WITCHCRAFT...

WHERE I SAW MONICA FOR THE LAST TIME...

WHERE DANI THOUGHT I...

IT'S WEIRD TO KNOW SO MUCH TIME HAS PASSED...

YOU'RE GONNA DIE, FOOLISH!

I'LL AVENGE MY SISTERS WHO DIED AT THE STAKE!!

NOOO, HELP!

HUH...

WHAT?!

...

WHAT A GAME...

MUAHAHA! YOU CAN'T RUN AWAY!

GET READY TO SUFFER MY WICKED MAGIC!

STOP, YOU EVIL WITCH!

YES, IT'S ACTUALLY ME!! QUEEN MONICA, THE GOOD WITCH!! I'VE COME TO RESCUE YOU!!

I'M A GOOD WITCH TOO, LOOK! I'VE GOT A WAND!

THANK YOU, QUEEN MONICA!

OOOOH!

YOUR POSH MAGIC CAN'T DEFEAT ME, LITTLE PRINCESS!

I'M NOT A PRINCESS, I'M A QUEEN!

AND YOU FELL INTO MY TRAP!! COME ON, SERVANTS, THROW THE POTION AT HER!

NOOOO!

HA-HA!

DORIAN? WHAT ARE YOU DOING?!

COME ON!

AH, SORRY!

I'M COMING!

ACCORDING TO THE LOCALS, DANI WAS HERE.

YES, AND SHE DESTROYED THE CATHEDRAL!

THAT'S SCARY...

IT SEEMS THAT I ALWAYS ARRIVE TOO LATE.

DON'T FEEL DISCOURAGED, MAN. WE HAD TO TRY IT!

I TOLD YOU DANI WOULD BE AT THE WEDDING!

PUFF

WHOA! WHAT'S GOING ON?!

WITCHCRAFT!

THEY'RE SPIES OF QUEEN DANI!

WHAT THE...?!

WOOOW!

AHA! NOW YOU CAN FINALLY SEE MY REAL HEIGHT!

YOU'RE GOING TO BITE THE DUST, MARK! SEE WHO'S TALLER NOW!

...

...I DON'T WANT TO HEAR A WORD.

ANYWAY, THIS MUST MEAN THAT DANI IS HERE SOMEWHERE.

I ALWAYS GO BACK TO MY NORMAL SIZE WHEN SHE'S AROUND.

EH?

IT'S ME, DORIAN.

HUH, YES...

HIS VOICE.

IT SOUNDS SO DEEP!

BUT YES, IT'S REALLY HIM.

I'M SO SORRY...ABOUT DISAPPEARING FOR SO LONG.

I... MMMH...

THERE'S NO DOUBT.

THIS IS SO WEIRD...

I'VE DREAMT OF THIS MOMENT FOR SO LONG.

I JUST WANT TO HUG HIM AGAIN,

I WANNA CHECK IF HE'S TRULY ALIVE.

BUT...

WOULD THAT BE OK? HUGGING THIS PERSON?

HE LOOKS
SO DIFFERENT.
I FEEL WEIRD.

UH...
MONICA...

THIS...

THIS IS
NOT WHAT I WAS
EXPECTING...

EH? NO, OF
COURSE N...!

MONICA,
LOOK!!

THE SPELL
SUDDENLY
BROKE!!

I WONDER
WHAT IT FEELS
LIKE TO HUG
HIM.

ARE YOU
ANGRY?

NICO!! YOU'RE SO
HANDSOME AND
SUPER TALL!

I AM,
AM I NOT?

OH, I'M
SO GLAD!

HOW DID
YOU GO BACK
TO NORMAL?!

THAT'S WHY WE
WERE WONDERING IF
YOU HAD CAPTURED
DANI OR...

I DON'T
REALLY KNOW.
I DIDN'T DO
ANYTHING!

IF YOU HAD
HEALED HER OR
SOMETHING.

HI, MONICA!

ACTUALLY NO.
DANI RAN AWAY
BEFORE I COULD
DO ANYTHING...

I KNEW IT.

I DON'T
KNOW WHERE
SHE IS...

AW, HELLO
SWEET CARLO!
LONG TIME NO
SEE!

...

SHE
HATES ME.

WE NEED TO GET THIS OVER WITH ONCE AND FOR ALL!

UH... YOU'RE RIGHT.

LET'S SAVE HER.

WHAT A CLICHÉ.

THIS IS MY CHANCE TO GET OUT OF HERE.

BUT WITHOUT MY WAND, THOUGH...

MMH?

OH, COME ON...

CLICK

THEY'RE SO USELESS.

I COULD GET RID OF THEM ONCE AND FOR ALL, IF I WANTED TO.

IT'S TOO MUCH OF A MESS, THOUGH.

I'D BETTER NOT MAKE THINGS MORE COMPLICATED.

UH...

ALL RIGHT...

PERFECT.

BUT FIRST...

I NEED TO FIND DANI!

WHERE COULD SHE BE?

I THINK I'LL PAY A VISIT TO QUEEN MONICA...

123

130

I'M SO GLAD WE'RE TOGETHER AGAIN.

MUM... TONIGHT YOU'LL SLEEP IN MY ROOM.

DON'T TRY ANYTHING FUNNY. THE GUARDS WILL ESCORT US.

... FINE.

...

AH! OF COURSE!

NOW I KNOW WHY DANI'S CURSE BROKE TODAY!

DO YOU?

DANI CURSED ME A LONG TIME AGO IN ORDER TO PROTECT ME FROM HER MOTHER!

NOW THAT SHE HAS LOST HER POWERS, I'M NO LONGER IN DANGER!

WHAT DID YOU CALL ME?

HOW UNBELIEVABLY SMART OF YOU, NICO!

WHAT DO YOU MEAN, UNBELIEVABLY?!

WHERE DID MONICA GO?

SHE WAS A BIT WEIRD...

MONICA...?

WHAT'S WRONG?!

ARE YOU ALL RIGHT?!

DORIAN...!

YOU'RE SO PALE! ARE YOU FEELING DIZZY?

I'M FINE, I'M FINE!

BUT...!

DON'T TOUCH ME!

135

136

AS SOON AS I FIND DANI, WE'LL REBUILD EVERYTHING TOGETHER.

PHEW...

OH... ARE YOU FEELING BETTER?

YES... WAY BETTER.

AH, UM... SORRY FOR HUGGING YOU LIKE THAT.

I SAW YOU WERE VERY NERVOUS, AND I THOUGHT YOU WERE HAVING A PANIC ATTACK.

YES...

THANK YOU SO MUCH, DORIAN.

PLEASE... LET ME STAY LIKE THIS FOR A FEW MOMENTS.

...

I DON'T THINK WILLIAM WILL BE HAPPY ABOUT IT.

CHAPTER 68

I'M TIRED, DAD! AND I'M HUNGRY! LET'S GO HOME AND EAT MAMA'S SOUP!

PATIENCE, ROBERT!

TOMORROW I'LL GO TO THE VILLAGE, AND I'M SURE PLENTY OF PEOPLE WILL WANT TO BUY A LOT OF FIREWOOD!

IT SEEMS THAT THE COLD WEATHER IS GONNA COME BACK IN THE NEXT COUPLE OF DAYS.

WELL, THAT'S WHY! IT'S SO COLD. WE SHOULD BE AT HOME DRINKING HOT SOUP!

UGH!

DADDY?! WHY HAVE YOU STOPPED ALL OF A SUDDEN?!

THERE'S... THERE'S SOMEONE IN THE DARK...

AH, THAT'S TRUE...

IT'S A GIRL!

GOOD EVENING, LADY! ARE YOU ALL RIGHT?!

COME TO OUR SHELTER! WE'VE GOT HOT SOUP!

AND LOTS OF FIREWOOD!

AND WHERE COULD WE FIND THE LUMBERJACK, GUYS?

DO YOU BELIEVE WHAT THEY'RE SAYING?

WHAT ARE YOU DOING, AISHA?

IT'S THE ONLY CLUE THAT WE'VE GOT AT THE MOMENT.

DID YOU HEAR THAT, MONICA? DANI IS EATING KIDS NOW.

CAN YOU PLEASE STOP STARING AND POINTING AT THEM, WILLIAM?

WE'RE SUPPOSED TO GO UNNOTICED.

...

HEY, DORIAN...

I'VE ALSO SEEN HER WITH RED EYES, AND IT CLEARLY WASN'T HER.

SHE WAS SORT OF POSSESSED.

THE REAL DANI'S STILL THERE AND WE CAN SAVE HER.

YOU HEARD THAT, RIGHT? DANI IS IN THE MOUNTAINS.

YES...

BUT IF THEY'RE ALREADY SCARED OF WITCHES, FLYING UP THERE WOULD BE DANGEROUS.

HOW CAN WE GET THERE WITHOUT BEING SEEN?

LEAVE IT TO ME AND MARK.

♪♫

♪

AW! YOU LOOK SO HAPPY, MONICA!

I HAVEN'T HEARD YOU SING IN A WHILE!

INDEED, THREE YEARS TO BE PRECISE.

IT MUST BE THE HAPPINESS OF THE NEWLY MARRIED!

YEEEAH, SURE THING...

UGH!

HEY, DORIAN. ARE YOU OK, DUDE?

... I'M SCARED...

DO YOU WANNA SEE SOMETHING REALLY COOL?

OH! A CRYSTAL BALL!

I GOT IT FROM MONICA'S SECRET LABORATORY!

DO YOU WANT ME TO TRY TO SEE THE FUTURE...?

EH, BLOODY! DON'T BE SO SELFISH AND LEAVE SOME FOOD FOR CARLO!

BAD DRAGON, BAD DRAGON!

BLOODY? HIS NAME IS NOT BLOODY!

HMM?

HAVE YOU ALREADY GIVEN HIM A NAME?

YES! HIS NAME IS DONATO!

DONATO THE DRAGON!

DORIAN, THAT'S NOT A DRAGON NAME AT ALL!

EH? WELL, I THINK IT SUITS HIM... BESIDES, HE LIKES IT. ISN'T THAT RIGHT, DONATO?

THAT'S TRUE, HE LIKES IT.

HUFF...

HA...

I'M SO TIRED...

HOW LONG HAVE WE BEEN CLIMBING?

I TOLD YOU IT WAS GONNA RAIN!

AND WHAT DID YOU EXPECT US TO DO?!

WE HAD TO CLIMB THE MOUNTAIN!

IF ONLY DORIAN WASN'T SO SLOW!

I DO... WHAT I CAN.

STOP FIGHTING! WE NEED TO TAKE COVER!

AH!

LOOK, OVER THERE! IT'S THE LUMBERJACK'S SHELTER!

WE'VE ARRIVED!

IT SEEMS LIKE SOMETHING MUST HAVE SCARED THEM A LOT...

YEAH...

GOOD NEWS, THEN.

DANI IS HERE SOMEWHERE.

HUH... BUT... LOOK AT THE WINDOWS...

KNOCK KNOCK KNOCK

145

ME TOO.

SOB
SOB

GUYS, GET INSIDE! LET'S HAVE DINNER!

AND SHUT THE DOOR, OR THE COLD GETS IN.

YES! I'M SORRY, MADAM!

THANK YOU SO MUCH! IT SMELLS SO GOOD!

YEAH, WELL... ABOUT WHAT YOU WERE ASKING, GUYS...

IT'S TRUE, WE SAW A WITCH IN THE MIDDLE OF THE MOUNTAIN, AT NIGHT...

149

LOOK! I'VE GOT A CRYSTAL BALL!

I HAVEN'T USED IT IN A LONG TIME. I HOPE IT'LL WORK! COME ON, SHOW ME HOW WE'RE GONNA RESCUE DANI!

AWESOME!

GOOD IDEA, NICO!

AH... I CAN SEE SOMETHING...

WOOO!! WHAT DO YOU SEE?!

EH?

WHAT A CRAPPY CRYSTAL BALL!!

EH?

REALLY?! IN SHORTS?!

IT SHOWED DORIAN WITH A PAIR OF SHORTS!!

PERHAPS THE BALL IS SUGGESTING THAT WE'LL SAVE DANI IN SUMMER?

WELL, IT'S DECEMBER NOW, SO...

SHORTS...

HOW WEIRD...

YAWN

COME ON, GET IN BED, EVERYONE! YOU MUST BE EXHAUSTED!

YOU CAN SLEEP IN THE BUNK BEDS!

THANK YOU SO MUCH!

WOULD IT BE POSSIBLE TO HAVE A PRIVATE ROOM FOR MY WIFE AND I? WE'RE NEWLY WED, YOU KNOW...?

AH...!

NO, NO, PLEASE DON'T BOTHER. SERIOUSLY! I PREFER TO SLEEP IN THE BUNK BEDS WITH THE OTHERS!

...

IT'S SETTLED: I'LL FIX YOU THE BEST ROOM OF THE HOUSE!

DARN YOU, WILLIAM! WHAT A SETUP!!

UGHHHH

FOLLOW ME, I'LL PREPARE THE BEDS.

HUH...?

THE BALL IS SHOWING ME SOMETHING...

BUT THIS...

THIS IS THE DAY DANI SAW DORIAN AT THE STAKE...

THE LAST TIME I SAW DANI...

AS SHE USED TO BE...

STOP!

WHAT KIND OF JOKE IS THIS?

WHY IS THE BALL SHOWING THE PAST...?

I WANT THE UPPER BED!

ME TOO!

I WANT THIS ONE.

ARE YOU SERIOUS? DID YOU LEAVE ME OUT?

GOOD NIGHT, EVERYONE!

PILLOW FIGHT?!

HA-HA!

NICO, THAT'S NOT FUNNY! I ALMOST BUMPED AGAINST THE WOOD!

NOW THAT I THINK ABOUT IT, I DON'T WANNA SLEEP WITH A BUNCH OF KIDS...

THERE'S ANOTHER ROOM LIKE THIS ONE JUST ACROSS THE HALL.

I THINK I'M GONNA TAKE A BATH...

FINE, I'LL WAIT FOR YOU IN BED!

... WITH DORIAN...? THAT BRAT...?

UH... I'M IN LOVE WITH HIM!

I'M...!

AND I...

I WANT...

!

WILLIAM, WAIT!

... UH... WHAT DID I JUST SAY?

TO ANNUL THE MARRIAGE?

SHE'S IN LOVE WITH DORIAN?

IN LOVE?!

WHEN DID THAT HAPPEN?!

WHAT THE HELL IS WRONG WITH MONICA?!

CAN'T SHE UNDERSTAND THAT SHE'S THE QUEEN?!

WE NEED TO FULFILL OUR OBLIGATIONS!

THAT'S WHAT OUR PARENTS TOLD US!!

THAT'S WHAT THE WHOLE KINGDOM IS EXPECTING OF US!

WHY DOES SHE WANT TO THROW IT ALL AWAY...?!

WHY?!

ONLY BECAUSE SHE WANTS TO BE WITH DORIAN?

I DON'T GET IT.

WHAT DO YOU WANT, WILL?

IT'S MY DUTY TO MARRY MONICA.

TO BE HER HUSBAND.

TO BE THE KING.

WHAT'S ON YOUR MIND?

WHAT DO YOU WANT?

...

WOW... IT LOOKS LIKE THERE'S PLENTY OF PEOPLE IN THIS HOUSE...

GOOD...

KILL THEM.

LET ONLY ONE LIVE.

IT'LL BE GOOD...

...

ALL RIGHT.

DANI!

IT'S ME, DORIAN!

DANI, SAY SOMETHING!

WHAT'S GOING ON?

WHY ARE YOU BEING SO LOUD?!

IT'S YOUR SISTER!!

WHAT?!

DORIAN...

I THINK SHE...

SHE CAN'T RECOGNIZE ME...

I DON'T KNOW WHAT SORT OF REACTION I WAS EXPECTING FROM HER, BUT...

SHE ISN'T RESPONDING AT ALL.

THAT...

WAKE UP!

I'M SORRY IT TOOK ME SO LONG TO COME FOR YOU, DANI, I...!

I SHOULD HAVE BEEN BY YOUR SIDE!

BUT I'M BEGGING YOU, SAY SOMETHING!

RESPOND! DANI...!

CHANGE OF PLANS...

...

WHAT DO YOU WANT?

166

WE CAN'T JUST SIT HERE AND WAIT!

WE MUST HELP THEM!

I AGREE WITH WILL, FOR ONCE!

THEY MIGHT NEED US!

YES, WE MUST HELP DORIAN!

WHERE DID YOU FIND THAT, AISHA?!

DON'T YOU DARE TOUCH DANI WITH IT!

GUYS... BE CAREFUL.

YES, MUCH STRENGTH TO YOU!

GOOD LUCK, WITCHES!

ARE THEY ALSO GONNA FLY ON A BROOM, MUMMY?

THANK YOU SO MUCH FOR EVERYTHING.

AND WE'RE SORRY FOR WHAT HAPPENED.

LATER WE'LL COME BACK TO FIX THE SHELTER. I PROMISE!

DANI, LOOK AT ME!

IT'S ME, DORIAN!

I'M YOUR BROTHER!

LOOK CLOSELY, WE LOOK A LOT LIKE EACH OTHER!

... BROTHER?

YES, IT'S ME!

DO YOU REMEMBER ME NOW?!

UGH...

COME ON, GET UP. I WILL TAKE YOU TO THE OTHERS.

TOGETHER, WE WILL FIND A WAY FOR YOU TO GET BETTER.

NO...

I WON'T LET YOU TAKE HER AWAY...

WHEW, YOU'VE ALSO GROWN UP A LOT!

YOU'RE AS TALL AS NICO! OR MAYBE A BIT MORE...?

UH...

DANI?

HUH?

175

WHAT
ARE YOU
DOING?!

DA...!

WHAT IS
GOING ON?!

...NI...

UH...

RED EYES.

FOCUS,
DORIAN.

WHAT
HAVE YOU
READ ABOUT
RED EYES?

NOT THIS...

OR THIS...

NO, THIS ISN'T USEFUL...

BUT THERE'S SOMETHING...

DEEP DOWN...

I REMEMBER SOMETHING...

HEY, DORIAN...

I'VE ALSO SEEN HER WITH RED EYES, AND IT CLEARLY WASN'T HER.

SHE WAS SORT OF POSSESSED.

BOOM

SHE'S POSSESSED! AN EVIL SPIRIT LIES WITHIN HER...

MONICA WAS RIGHT.

DANI HASN'T BECOME EVIL!

AND I KNOW HOW TO GET IT OUT!

STAY AWAY, DANI!

MONICA, GO GET DORIAN!

YES!

WE NEED TO GET HIM OUT OF HERE RIGHT NOW.

THE BARRIER WON'T HOLD FOR MUCH LONGER!

... THEY SEEM TO HAVE EVERYTHING UNDER CONTROL...

WHAT DO YOU THINK, CARLO?

DORIAN!

YOU WERE RIGHT ABOUT DANI!

SHE'S NOT EVIL OR CRAZY!

I DISCOVERED SHE'S JUST POS--

DORIAN!

WHAT HAPPENED?!

WHERE'S KING WILLIAM?

!

AH... DANI'S OVER THERE!

OH NO... TELL ME HE'S OKAY...

WILLIAM!! ARE YOU THERE?!

MAJESTY!

WHERE IS SHE GOING?

...

WE SHOULD FOLLOW HER!

WHAT ABOUT WILLIAM? WHERE IS HE?

WE'RE OVER HERE!

MONICA!! ARE YOU OK?!

YES, WE'RE FINE!

HE FAINTED.

SHE WOULDN'T HURT HIM.

WE CAN'T BE SURE.

BUT YOU MUST HURRY TO HELP DORIAN. I THINK DANI HURT HIM.

ALSO, DORIAN SEEMS TO HAVE FOUND OUT SOMETHING! WHEN I SAW HIM HE LOOKED SO HAPPY!

GREAT.

OH, AND NICO...

BE CAREFUL. I BELIEVE IN YOU!

THAT'S MY LINE.

TREAD CAREFULLY, QUEEN MONICA.

I WON'T BE ABLE TO BE YOUR BODYGUARD THIS TIME.

DON'T WORRY ABOUT ME. I CAN TAKE CARE OF MYSELF.

193

DAMIEN.

HUH?

...

WHAT? WHAT IS IT?

YOU'RE NOT LEAVING EITHER, ARE YOU?

WILL WE STILL BE FRIENDS, THE THREE OF US?

WAIT, WHAT?

WHAT DO YOU MEAN, "FRIENDS"?

YOU TWO AREN'T FRIENDS...

WELL, ACTUALLY, WE ARE.

MONICA JUST TOLD ME SHE ONLY WANTS TO BE MY FAKE WIFE.

DON'T TELL ANYONE THOUGH!

WHOA... COOL...

WELL, YEAH... HE'S QUITE IMPRESSIVE...

THANK YOU SO MUCH, DAMIEN! YOU RULE!

COME ON, YOU GUYS! THE OTHERS NEED OUR HELP!

WHY DID WILLIAM LOOK AT ME THAT WAY? WHAT IS THAT IDIOT THINKING?

AAAARGH, I'M THE REAL IDIOT HERE. I'M WAY TOO HAPPY.

NO, NO, NO, DAMIEN. NOW IS NOT THE TIME.

YOUR CLUMSY SIBLINGS NEED TO BE RESCUED BEFORE THEY GET HURT FOR REAL.

KEEP A CLEAR HEAD!

TAKE IT, DAMIEN!

AH!

HURRY UP, WILL! GET ON MY BROOM!

DON'T WORRY, I'LL GET ON DAMIEN'S BROOM. IT'S NOT THE FIRST TIME HE'S TAKEN ME AS A COPILOT!

CLEAR HEAD. CLEAR HEAD.

!

WHILE WE'RE FLYING YOU CAN GIVE ME LOVE ADVICE, DAMIEN.

NOW THAT I'M SINGLE AGAIN.

IF YOU DON'T SHUT UP, I'LL THROW YOU OFF THE BROOM, YOU FOOL.

DAMIEN. I WANT TO TELL YOU SOMETHING BEFORE WE CONFRONT DANI AGAIN.

I BROUGHT THIS TO USE IN CASE IT IS NECESSARY.

IT'S... THE POTION I USED ON YOUR MOTHER, YES.

TO END HER MAGICAL POWERS FOREVER.

I CAN THROW IT AWAY IF YOU WANT. I'M NOT SURE IF I WAS RIGHT TO BRING IT.

NO, KEEP IT.

JUST IN CASE.

UGH...

THIS STUPID BODY ONCE AGAIN...

I NEED TO GAIN STRENGTH...OR THAT SPOILED BRAT WON'T LET ME USE HERS...

AH! YOU FINALLY APPEARED!

ABOUT TIME!

HAVEN'T YOU NOTICED?!

?

LOOK, KILL THEM ALL AND LET'S GET OUT OF HERE.

I WAS DOING SO WELL, BEING A GIANT SNAKE...

HEY... THEY'RE AFTER YOU!

I'M BORED OUT OF MY HEAD. THESE PEOPLE ARE TIRING.

... ALL RIGHT.

DANI...

AH! LOOK! DORIAN'S OVER THERE!

SHE SAW US!

TRUE. I HOPE HE'S FIN--

UGH!

201

WHAT DO YOU MEAN? WHAT'S HAPPENING TO YOU?

YOUR MOTHER IS NO LONGER HERE TO BOSS YOU AROUND.

WHY ARE YOU DOING THIS?

WHY WERE YOU GONNA KILL MARK?

BECAUSE HE TELLS ME TO DO IT.

HE?

WHO ARE YOU TALK...?

DANI WAS SO COOL. IT'S SUCH A SHAME THAT SHE WENT CRAZY! WHATEVER, THERE'S NOTHING TO DO!

YES, IT LOOKS LIKE EVERYTHING'S GOING GREAT. WE'VE KILLED TWO BIRDS WITH ONE STONE AND WITHOUT GETTING OUR HANDS DIRTY.

I WANT TO GO BACK TO THE PALACE. I NEVER THOUGHT MY FAMILY WOULD PERSECUTE ME FOR SO LONG! WHAT A NIGHTMARE!

THERE'S A REASON WHY I GOT OUT OF THERE. YEAH, IT MUST BE HARD TO BE BLOOD BOUND TO SUCH TWISTED PEOPLE.

SLAM

AH, DORIAN...

DORIAN! WHAT ARE YOU DOING HERE?

DID YOU ACTUALLY HEAR...?

THIS IS STUPID. IT MAKES NO SENSE.

I DON'T KNOW WHO YOU ARE, BUT YOU'RE NOT MY FRIENDS.

HMM... I'D SAY THIS DOOR WASN'T HERE BEFORE...

WHERE ARE YOU GOING, DORIAN?

I'M LOOKING FOR DANI.

SOMETHING TELLS ME SHE'S REALLY CLOSE...

... WHO'S THAT?

HMM...?

AH... YOU.

HI, SON.

IT'S BEEN A LONG TIME.

I'M GLAD TO SEE YOU'VE GROWN UP...

YOU RESEMBLE ME A LOT!

EVEN THOUGH I WOULD NEVER HAVE BETRAYED MY OWN FAMILY TO THE POINT OF KILLING MY FATHER.

YOU'VE GOT SOME AUDACITY, DORIAN...

IN THE END, YOU'RE THE MOST TWISTED AMONG US...

HUH?

I'VE GOT NO TIME FOR SUCH SILLINESS.

I KNOW YOU'RE NOT MY REAL FATHER, AND ALL OF THIS SOUNDS LIKE A BAD JOKE.

I NEED TO FIND DANI. LEAVE ME ALONE.

WHERE DO YOU THINK YOU'RE GOING?! MURDERER!

YOU'VE KILLED ME! YOU'LL NEVER FIND DANI!

HEY...

HELLO, SWEETHEART...

STOP IT, SERIOUSLY. THE MORE YOU TRY, THE MORE I REMEMBER THIS PLACE.

IT'S NOT THE FIRST TIME YOU TRIED TO SCARE ME.

YOU'RE NOT MY REAL MOTHER.

RIGHT, YOUR MOTHER IS ALONE, LOCKED UP IN THAT COLD PALACE, SURROUNDED BY ENEMIES AND DEPRIVED OF HER POWERS.

YOU'VE ABANDONED HER. HAVEN'T YOU, DORIAN?

THAT'S NOT TRUE! YOU DON'T KNOW ME!

YOU THINK YOU CAN LOOK THROUGH ME,

THAT YOU CAN CONTROL AND TERRIFY ME WITH CHEAP TRICKS.

IT'S SIMPLE, THOUGH. YOU DON'T KNOW A SINGLE THING. I WON'T ABANDON MY MOTHER.

OR DANI.

I DON'T KNOW HOW I ENDED UP HERE, BUT I REMEMBER I CAME FOR HER.

I'LL GET HER OUT OF THIS PLACE, AND WE'LL BE TOGETHER AGAIN, AS A FAMILY. ALL OF US.

STOP FOLLOWING ME.

214

DORIAN, DON'T GET DISTRACTED. DANI'S PROBABLY TRAPPED SOMEWHERE.

I NEED TO GET HER OUT OF HERE, NO MATTER WHAT.

AH!

DANI!

... DORIAN?

WAAAH!

WHAT HAPPENED?

I'M SO GLAD YOU'RE HERE! WE NEED TO DO SOMETHING!

EVERYTHING... EVERYTHING'S GOING WRONG, DORIAN. WE NEED TO FIX THIS!

DON'T WORRY, DANI. EVERYTHING'S GONNA BE OK NOW.

NOW THAT I'VE FOUND YOU.

I'VE BEEN LOOKING FOR YOU FOR SO LONG.

THIS PLACE IS SO COLD AND LONELY...

IS THIS HOW YOU FEEL, DANI?

HAVE YOU BEEN ON YOUR OWN, LOCKED UP IN HERE ALL THIS TIME?

DORIAN...

I'M SO SORRY...

I'M GLAD YOU'RE HERE.

YOU'LL STAY WITH ME NOW. AND I WON'T BE ALONE ANYMORE!

HUH?

STAY?

BUT I DIDN'T COME TO STAY.

ARE...

ARE YOU GONNA LEAVE AGAIN?

NO!

I MEAN... YES, BUT YOU'RE COMING WITH ME, DANI.

WHERE?

WHAT DO YOU MEAN, WHERE?

WELL... AH...

THINK, DORIAN...

WHERE?

HOW DID I GET HERE?

HOW COULD I FORGET?

WHAT WAS I DOING BEFORE?

I NEED TO TAKE DANI WITH ME AS SOON AS POSSIBLE.

BUT I BELIEVE... I BELIEVE I'VE BEEN HERE BEFORE...

DORIAN... ARE YOU ALL RIGHT?

WHERE AM I?

THOSE PEOPLE EARLIER WEREN'T DAD OR MUM... SOMEONE'S TRYING TO FOOL ME. WHAT FOR?

...

HEY, TELL ME...

YOU'RE NOT REAL EITHER, ARE YOU?

WRETCHED...

KID...!

AAAAAH!

LET ME GO!

ARGH...

UGH...

GET OUT OF ME!

THE CAT...

IT'S NOT THE CAT ANYMORE...

THE SPIRIT IS THERE!

I CAN DO THIS.

IT'S...

IT'S TOO EASY.

IN REALITY, THIS SPIRIT IS SO WEAK.

COULD IT BE...?

YES... THE POWER CAME FROM DANI ALL LONG.

BUT THEN...

WHAT HAPPENED TO YOU?

YOU'RE WAY MORE POWERFUL THAN I AM.

DANI...?

UH...

WHAT DO I LOOK LIKE?

SUPER HANDSOME.

COOL!

DANI... ARE YOU OK?

HOW ARE YOU FEELING? CAN YOU REMEMBER ME?

...

... NO.

WHAT ABOUT ME? REMEMBER ME?

YES, NICO.

CAN YOU REMEMBER HOW WE MET?

... YOU WERE...IN THE DARK CASTLE.

...

WHAT ABOUT EVERYONE ELSE? CAN YOU REMEMBER ALL THESE PEOPLE?

... NO.

DAMIEN... WHAT'S GOING ON?

WHY DIDN'T IT WORK?

I DON'T KNOW.

DORIAN SUPPOSEDLY GOT RID OF THE EVIL SPIRIT THAT WAS POSSESSING HER, BUT...

DANI... TELL ME, WOULD YOU LIKE TO COME TO THE SHELTER WITH US?

ALL RIGHT.

GOOD...

COME ON, STAND UP!

226

IF IT'S HARD FOR YOU TO WALK, I'LL CARRY YOU!

YOU KNOW I CAN HANDLE YOUR WEIGHT. I'M STRONG NOW.

I CAN WALK.

OKAY... IT SEEMS LIKE SHE IS NO LONGER AGGRESSIVE NOW THAT THE SPIRIT IS GONE...

LET'S TAKE HER TO THE SHELTER.

WE ALL NEED SOME SLEEP.

AND A GOOD SHOWER! I'M PRETTY SURE WE STINK.

WE'LL TAKE CARE OF DANI THERE. COME ON!

UGH...

AH... DORIAN?

I...I'M SORRY!

I CAN'T... UGH...

HEY...

!

DORIAN, WAIT!

WHERE ARE YOU GOING?!

UUUGH...

UGH...

DORIAN...

HEY...

SHE DOESN'T REMEMBER, MONICA! SHE DOESN'T REMEMBER ME!

I THOUGHT I COULD SAVE HER...

BUT I COULDN'T DO ANYTHING.

OF COURSE YOU DID! SHE'S WITH US NOW.

SHE'S NOT! THAT'S NOT DANI!

SHE'S SAFE!

WE CAN BRING HER BACK, DORIAN.

WE'LL HEAL HER. ALL OF US.

WE'LL FIGURE OUT WHAT HAPPENED AND FIND A SOLUTION.

YOU DON'T GET IT, MONICA...

THE SPIRIT... BEFORE IT DISAPPEARED, IT TOLD ME...

IT TOLD ME DANI WASN'T COMING BACK,

THAT SOMETHING POWERFUL WAS HOLDING HER BACK...

AND ARE YOU GONNA TRUST AN EVIL SPIRIT?

IT FED ON PAIN, REMEMBER?

IT JUST WANTED TO HURT YOU.

...

UH... BUT HOW'S IT POSSIBLE...

THAT SHE DOESN'T REMEMBER ME?

MONICA...

I'M TIRED.

TONIGHT... DAMN, IT WAS SCARY.

YES...

AND YOU DIDN'T SEE THE GIANT SNAKE!

I PROMISE WE'LL FIND A SOLUTION.

TOGETHER.

UH...

THANK YOU...

FOR EVERYTHING.

SERIOUSLY, I...

AH...

I...

UH...

ARE YOU FEELING BETTER?

YES.

DO YOU WANT TO JOIN THE OTHERS?

NO.

THERE'S NOTHING IN THAT IMAGE APART FROM DANI, AND THAT WRETCHED CAT AND I!

AND THE CAT ISN'T A PROBLEM ANYMORE...

I'M OVERLOOKING SOMETHING HERE.

BUT WHAT?

DANI...

I'D BETTER DISCUSS THIS WITH THE OTHERS. MAYBE TOGETHER WE'LL DISCOVER SOMETHING...

AH...

IT'S WEIRD TO FINALLY HAVE HER HERE.

NOT FOR ME. I'VE LIVED LIKE THIS FOR THREE YEARS.

TO BE HONEST, IT FEELS LIKE WE'RE BACK TO THE STARTING POINT.

THAT SPIRIT ATTACHED ITSELF TO HER LIKE A TICK, TAKING ADVANTAGE OF HER WEAKNESS TO DOMINATE HER.

BUT WHAT MADE HER WEAK IN THE FIRST PLACE?

HERE, YOUNG LADY...

CAREFUL NOT TO CATCH A COLD.

YOU SHOULD GO INSIDE. I'M GOING TO GET BREAKFAST READY, IT'S GETTING LATE.

NOW THAT SHE MENTIONS IT...

IT'S CERTAINLY GETTING LATE.

WHERE ARE THOSE TWO?

UH...
WHAT TIME IS IT...?

DID I FALL ASLEEP...?

AH, DORIAN!

OH MY, OH MY.

WAAAAAA!

MONICA, I HAD A GREAT IDEA!

I KNOW HOW TO MAKE DANI REMEMBER ME.

I'VE GOT A BRILLIANT PLAN.

A PLAN?

YES! COME ON, STAND UP! WE NEED TO EXPLAIN MY PLAN TO EVERYONE!

COMING!

STOP COMPLAINING, AMIR. YOU HAVEN'T DONE ANYTHING USEFUL UNTIL NOW!

YOU'RE THE FEARLESS ONE, AISHA!

I'M NOT GOOD AT ANYTHING THAT IMPLIES MOVING FROM THE DIVAN, YOU KNOW THAT.

I GET THIS FROM MOTHER.

I CAN HEAR YOU.

SHUT UP AND COME. YOU'RE SO LAZY!

AISHA, YOU'VE JUST COME BACK AND YOU'RE LEAVING AGAIN?

MONICA NEEDS US!

TURNS OUT WE'LL BE SAVING THE DAY IN THE END.

DORIAN HAS A PLAN!

WE'LL GIVE DANI HER MEMORY BACK, AND WE NEED PEOPLE WHO KNEW HER THREE YEARS AGO!

SO COME ON, THERE'S NO TIME TO LOSE!

HELLO, PRINCESS MONICA! OH...YOUR MAJESTY, NOW? IT'S BEEN SO LONG!

HI, MR. EVANS! IS EVERYTHING ALL RIGHT?

YES, SHE'S TAKING A BATH.

DID YOU BRING HER CLOTHES?

YES... BUT LOOK AT THIS!

THIS IS UNACCEPTABLE!

THAT'S WHAT SHE WAS WEARING EARLIER, ISN'T IT?

YES! CAN YOU BELIEVE IT?!

DORIAN PERFORMED ONE OF THOSE SPELLS TO FIX THE DAMAGE, AND THAT'S IT!

I TOLD HIM DANI COULDN'T JUST GO AROUND DRESSED AS AN EVIL WITCH! NO WAY!

I EVEN OFFERED TO GO SHOPPING MYSELF!

SHOPPING...? IT SEEMS DIFFICULT, JUDGING BY THE STATE OF THE VILLAGE...

ALL BUSINESSES CLOSED WHEN THE WAR BROKE OUT.

THOUGH THERE IS A LADY WHO USED TO BE A DRESSMAKER...

THAT SOUNDS PERFECT!

ARE YOU GONNA DESIGN IT? CAN YOU DRAW?

TALKING TO YOURSELF AGAIN?

I'M TALKING TO DONATO.

MONICA SAYS THAT YOU NEED MY INVALUABLE HELP.

OF COURSE! I'M THE KEY TO SOLVING THE MYSTERY WHICH HOLDS DANI CAPTIVE.

THANK YOU FOR FINDING NICO, DESPITE HOW STUBBORN I GOT OVER DANI'S CLOTHES.

...

HEY, ARE YOU LISTENING?

OH, YEAH, I'M SORRY.

THAT'S RIGHT, I NEED YOUR HELP.

WHAT DO WE NEED TO DO, THEN?

WE NEED TO REBUILD MASTER PENDRAGON'S HOUSE, JUST AS IT WAS BEFORE THE FLAMES DESTROYED IT.

WE NEED TO BE PRECISE, CAREFUL THAT EACH DETAIL IS EXACTLY LIKE OLD TIMES.

THAT'S WHY I NEED TO MAKE A REBUILDING PLAN BETWEEN US THREE.

YOU LIVED HERE LONGER THAN ANYONE ELSE, NICO, SO I TRUST YOUR MEMORY.

CONSIDER IT DONE.

KING WILLIAM WENT LOOKING FOR BRICKS, STONE, WOOD...

MATERIALS THAT WE NEED TO RECONSTRUCT THE HOUSE.

IN THE MEANTIME, I SENT DAMIEN TO LOOK FOR A WAND, SINCE MINE BROKE.

I TOLD HIM TO BORROW IT FROM A NEIGHBOR.

MANY WITCHES LIVE IN THE AREA NOW; MAYBE SOMEONE WILL HELP US.

WHEN I WOKE UP AFTER THREE YEARS, I FELT VERY STRANGE.

EVERYTHING WAS DIFFERENT; WE HAD ALL GROWN UP ALL OF A SUDDEN.

PERHAPS THE SAME HAPPENED TO DANI.

MAYBE SHE DIDN'T RECOGNIZE ME 'CAUSE I'VE CHANGED TOO MUCH.

MAYBE IF WE MANAGE TO MAKE THIS WORLD RESEMBLE THE ONE SHE LOVED AND LEFT BEHIND...

MAYBE AT THAT POINT...

SHE'LL BE ABLE TO REMEMBER AND COME BACK.

SO, THE LAST PART OF THE PLAN, THE MOST IMPORTANT...

LEAVE IT TO ME, OF COURSE!

YAY! I'M SO HAPPY!

I WILL DO MY BEST!

I CAN'T BELIEVE WHAT I'M ABOUT TO SAY, BUT...

FOR ONCE, I TRUST THIS SILLY PLAN OF YOURS!

I'M SURE IT'LL WORK!

COME ON, LET'S GET TO WORK!

HEY, NICO... LISTEN... THANK YOU FOR SAYING THAT.

BUT YOU SHOULD STOP TORTURING YOURSELF.

I STILL LOVE MY PARENTS. I WANT MY MUM TO REDEEM HERSELF AND REBOOT HER LIFE,

DESPITE THE FACT THAT THEY STARTED A GRUESOME WAR AND TRIED TO INVOLVE THEIR OWN CHILDREN.

AND THEY KILLED MY PARENTS.

THAT'S RIGHT, THEY KILLED MONICA'S PARENTS.

THEY ALSO KILLED MANY NEIGHBORS IN THE VILLAGE, SOME OF MY FRIENDS' MOTHERS AND FATHERS, WHEN I WAS A LITTLE BOY.

IT WAS TRAUMATIZING.

AND BEFORE THAT, MY FATHER ORDERED YOUR MOTHER TO BE BURNED FOR SIMPLY BEING A WITCH.

I SUPPOSE HE'S TO BLAME FOR ALL OF THIS.

WELL, IN TRUTH, THE FIRST ONE WHO SENT HUNDREDS OF WITCHES TO THE STAKE WAS MY FATHER.

HE'S ALSO TO BE BLAMED...

MUM AND DAD SET ME AGAINST YOU. IT WAS ALL VERY CONFUSING AND...

NOW I DO SEE YOU'RE A GOOD PERSON, DAMIEN.

AND I'M NOT SCARED OF YOU ANYMORE.

YOU'RE THE ONLY OLDER BROTHER I'VE GOT, AND...

I'D LIKE FOR US TO REALLY BEHAVE LIKE BROTHERS FROM NOW ON.

DORIAN...

I'M SO SORRY I ABANDONED BOTH YOU AND DANI IN THAT HOUSE.

HUH?

I LEFT KNOWING THAT IT WAS A TOXIC PLACE. I LEFT YOU BEHIND.

I WAS A SCARED KID, AND...

AND I'M SELFISH. THAT'S THE TRUTH.

I'VE NEVER BEEN ABLE TO FORGIVE MYSELF.

I THOUGHT I WOULDN'T NEED TO FACE IT. I TRIED TO GET YOU OUT OF MY HEAD, PRETEND YOU DIDN'T EXIST.

BUT YOU'RE HERE NOW, SAYING THAT YOU WANNA FIX THINGS.

INCLUDING OUR FAMILY.

OF COURSE. IT'S ALL GETTING FIXED.

...

SHE LOOKS QUITE HARMLESS WHEN SHE'S ASLEEP.

AISHA!

WHEN DID YOU ARRIVE?

A FEW HOURS AGO.

THE OTHERS ARE DOWNSTAIRS, EMPTYING YOUR FATHER'S CUPBOARD.

ARE... ARE YOU SURE WE'RE ALLOWED TO EAT ALL THESE CAKES?

IF ANYONE ASKS YOU, JUST SAY YOU HAVEN'T SEEN ANYTHING.

WE'VE BEEN HAVING DINNER AT THE MASTER'S HOUSE.

YOU SHOULD HAVE COME, AISHA!

YEAH, YOUR FATHER TOLD ME...

I DON'T KNOW. I DIDN'T WANT TO BOTHER YOU BY JOINING THE GROUP WITHOUT WARNING...

AH...

SO CUUUTE!

HEY!

YOU WERE WEARING THOSE SHORTS THE FIRST TIME I SAW YOU. REMEMBER?

I USED TO CALL YOU FROG-KID!

YES... AND I TRIED TO IMPRESS YOU... HOW PATHETIC.

OH, BUT YOU IMPRESSED AND ALSO SCARED ME.

I NOTICED I EARNED YOUR ADMIRATION WHEN YOU STOPPED CALLING ME FROG-KID,

AND YOU STARTED CALLING ME PROFESSOR WYTTE.

AAAAAH! WHAT ARE YOU TALKING ABOUT!

YOU'RE NOT CUTE ANYMORE!

HEY, YOU TWO!

DING DONG

SHE'S HERE!

COMING! WAIT A MINUTE!

DING DONG

MAKE SURE TO OPEN THE DOOR FROM THE FLOOR, MAJESTY!

YES!

AND CRYING! CRYING IS VERY IMPORTANT!

SEE YOU SOON!

DING DONG

GOOD LUCK!

DING DONG

OH, HI CARLO!

DO YOU KNOW YOUR LINES, BUDDY?

AH...

HELLO...

YOU'RE FINALLY HERE!

WELCOME!

...

COME ON IN, COME ON IN.

YOUR BROTHER'S WAITING FOR YOU INSIDE.

HERE, HAVE A SEAT, YOUNG LADY.

GREAT.

I'M GONNA MAKE YOU SOME HOT CHOCOLATE NOW, KIDS.

AHEM...

WHAT A MESS, HUH DANI?

IT WAS SUCH BAD LUCK, MISSING OUR SCHOOL BUS LIKE THAT!

WE'RE HOPELESS!

... BUS?

THERE YOU GO, KIDS.

THANKS.

UH...

PRINCE WILLIAM, REMEMBER YOUR LINE: "I ACCEPT YOU BOTH AS..."

OH, RIGHT!

...

CHILDREN, I ACCEPT YOU BOTH AS APPRENTICES...

TO FIGHT AGAINST THE EVIL WITCHES!

COOL!

SLURP

DING DONG

OPEN THE DOOR, MASTER!

PRINCESS MONICA'S HERE TO TALK TO YOU!

WELCOME, MY DEAR PRINCESS MONICA!

HI THERE!

AH... HELLO...

LET ME INTRODUCE MYSELF.

I'M DORIAN, HEIR OF THE WYTTE FAMILY.

AH... WHAT A CUTE KID!

...

HI DANI!

HELLO, NICO.

WHAT'S GOING ON?

SINCE PRINCESS MONICA'S HERE, WE'LL NEED TO BE CAREFUL NOT TO DO MAGIC!

SHE HATES WITCHES!

WHOOSH

DORIAN. THIS IS NOT WORKING.

WAIT.

CAN YOU REMEMBER THIS ROOM?

I USED TO SLEEP HERE,

AND YOU USED TO COME HERE WHEN YOU COULDN'T SLEEP.

COME ON, DANI! LET'S GO UPSTAIRS!

THIS IS WHERE WE REHEARSE OUR DANCE STEPS!

LOOK AT THAT! DO YOU REMEMBER IT?

HEY, DANI.

WHAT?

ARE YOU UP FOR A RACE?

A RACE?

YES.

DON'T YOU ENJOY FLYING?

LET'S GO!

DON'T BE A COWARD, DANI!

WE'RE GONNA FLY ON A BROOM!

ALL RIGHT.

AWESOME!

YOU'RE GOING DOWN!

YOU'LL SEE HOW QUICK I AM, DANI!

SPLASH!

AAAH!

WHAT'S THAT?!

DANI!

A MONSTER!

HURRY UP, WE NEED A BROOM!

OKAY!

278

OH NO!

SHE'S GONNA DROWN!

NICO, GET HER OUT OF THERE!

ARGH!

I NEED TO DO SOMETHING!

CARLO!

THERE YOU GO, DAMIEN.

DORIAN, TAKE THE BROOM.

NO, I WON'T BE OF ANY HELP WITH THAT.

I ACTUALLY NEED IT.

THANKS, DAMIEN.

IF ONLY I KNEW HOW TO USE A BOW...

AT LEAST I COULD HELP A LITTLE.

THROW SOME ROCKS AT THE MONSTER.

AISHA...

AS FAR AS I'M CONCERNED,

YOU'D BE AS USEFUL AS I AM, RIGHT NOW.

DAMIEN'S SPELLS AREN'T WORKING...

THIS LOOKS BAD...

OUT OF THE WAY!

!

WAIT, MONICA! WHAT ARE YOU GONNA DO?

YOU CAN'T CAST SPELLS!

WAIT!

UGH!

IT SEEMS THAT DAMIEN'S SPELLS AREN'T HURTING THE MONSTER AT ALL!

NEITHER ARE THE ARROWS.

PERHAPS IF I FREEZE THE WATER SURROUNDING IT, IT'LL BE PARALYZED.

NO!

OH NO...!

THERE'S SOMETHING STRANGE HERE.

WE ATTACKED THE CREATURE WITH SPELLS AND ARROWS... BUT THERE'S NOT A SINGLE SCRATCH.

DID IT REALLY DIE JUST FROM WILLIAM'S ATTACK?!

IS IT A SEA SNAKE?

WHOA, IT'S HUGE!

IT ATE THE KING!

AISHA! WHERE ARE YOU GOING?!

TO THE BATTLEFIELD!

WE'LL BE MORE USEFUL THERE!

GET OUT OF THE WAY, PLEASE!

LET ME THROUGH!

DON'T WORRY, WILL. I'M SURE I'VE GOT SOME POTION...

TO MAKE IT PUKE OR SOMETHING...?

MONICA GET AWAY FROM THERE!

IT'S DANGEROUS!

LET ME GO, DORIAN!

I NEED TO HELP WILL!

DORIAN'S RIGHT.

THIS IS REALLY ODD.

NICO...

DO YOU THINK IT HAS SWALLOWED DANI?

NO IDEA...

BUT LOOK AT ALL THAT SMOKE...

MAYBE THE MONSTER IS GOING TO EXPLODE.

WE MUST TAKE COVER NOW.

BUT WE NEED TO HELP WILL!

LEAVE THAT TO ME.

... DAMIEN?

I'M GONNA GET WILL OUT OF THERE.

I'LL OPEN THE SERPENT FROM TOP TO BOTTOM, IF NECESSARY.

AH... WAIT, NO...

THAT'S NOT SAFE EITH--

I'LL HELP YOU!

MONICA, THE SMOKE...!

EVERYBODY GET OUT OF THE WAY,

THINGS MIGHT GET DANGEROUS.

--DAMIEN, WAIT!

AH?!

WHY DID HE DO THAT?

WHY DID WILL SACRIFICE HIMSELF WITH NO HESITATION...?

IS HE DOING THAT BADLY?

AM I THAT BLIND?

WELL, IT DOESN'T MATTER RIGHT NOW...

I'M COMING TO SAVE YOU, WILL.

DAMIEN!

LOOK...

WHAT THE...?

WATCH OUT, DAMIEN.

WHOAAAA!

HOW?!

WHERE DID YOU COME FROM?!

YOU ALMOST STUCK THE SWORD IN MY FOREHEAD.

WILL! YOU'RE FINE!

HE HE, YEAH, TURNS OUT THE MONSTER IS NOT A REAL ONE.

...

I WAS LUCKY ENOUGH TO FALL INTO THE WATER.

THAT WAS SCARY...!

I WAS IN A SEA MADE OF TENTACLES COVERING MY EYES,

ALTHOUGH I WASN'T ABLE TO TOUCH THEM.

I'M GLAD HE'S FINE...

BUT THIS IS REALLY CONFUSING.

DAMIEN!

ARE YOU CRYING?!

UH...

UGH...

COME HERE, GIVE ME A HUG!

I'LL COMFORT YOU!

NO WAY!

IT'S YOUR FAULT. YOU'RE SUCH AN IDIOT!

LOOK, IT'S TRUE!

THE MONSTER IS JUST A MIRAGE!

I CAN WALK THROUGH IT LIKE IT'S NOTHING!

BUT... WHO WOULD DO SUCH A THING?

AND...WHY?

THAT'S WHY IT HASN'T DESTROYED THE HOUSE OR ANYTHING ELSE!

...

...

DORIAN!

AH...!

DANI...!

THEY'VE USED THE MONSTER AS A DISTRACTION!

WITCHES, CLEARLY.

AND WE STUPIDLY FELL FOR IT.

WE MUST FIND HER, BEFORE THEY TAKE HER TOO FAR AWAY!

I WON'T LOSE DANI AGAIN!

I THINK SOMEONE TOOK HER!

AH!

DANI!

THEY'RE TAKING HER AWAY!

PERHAPS THEY'RE TAKING HER TO SAVE HER FROM THE MONSTER.

HEY, MARK, OVER HERE!

BARRY! WHERE'D YOU COME FROM?

THESE WITCHES ARE WELL-KNOWN FOLLOWERS OF ANGELA AND HANS...

THEY ATTEMPTED TO CANCEL OUR NEWSPAPER MULTIPLE TIMES.

WE TRIED TO STOP THEM, AND IF IT WASN'T FOR NOAH,

I'M PRETTY SURE THE WITCHES WOULD BE MILES AWAY BY NOW.

ARE YOU OKAY?

YEAH... I'M FINE...

WE DON'T WANNA HURT YOU!

JUST LEAVE US ALONE.

LET US GO AND IT'LL ALL BE FINE.

BOOM

ARGH!

SARAH! ARE YOU ALL RIGHT?!

OH, COME ON!

WHO...?

IT'S FUNNY.

'CAUSE IF YOU WON'T GIVE MY SISTER BACK...

I DO INTEND TO HURT YOU QUITE A BIT.

LISTEN, BOB, THAT GUY... THAT GUY'S A WYTTE.

THE OLDER BROTHER IS ALSO THERE... AND THEY'VE GOT LOTS OF ARMED PEOPLE TOO.

KAT.

STOP IT.

WE WON'T LET YOU KIDNAP HER!

KIDNAP HER?

SHE'S MY SISTER!

SHE'S OUR QUEEN!

AISHA, WILLIAM, FOLLOW ME!

RIGHT NOW?!

THEY'VE ALREADY FALLEN OFF THEIR BROOMS, I CAN FINALLY HERD THEM AS WELL!

YES, RIGHT NOW!

...

AH!

DANI!

NICO, FOLLOW THEM!

GET RID OF THOSE TWO AND HIDE DANI IN A SAFE PLACE.

WAAAH, MUM, I DON'T LIKE THE NOISE!

HONEY, DON'T CRY.

THERE'S SO MUCH NOISE OUTSIIIDE!

DON'T BE AFRAID.

THE WITCHES WILL PROTECT US.

AH...

MARK, I'M ALSO AFRAID!

AISHA, WHAT ARE YOU LOOKING FOR?

ARROWS!

MONICA TOLD ME TO LOOK FOR ARROWS AND COVER THE TIPS WITH CLOTH.

AH!

THINGS ARE GETTING SERIOUS OUT THERE!

I'M GONNA GO OUT TO SEE IF I CAN HELP.

AHA! HERE THEY ARE!

HE HE...

THEY ALL HAVE THEIR FEET ON THE GROUND.

NOW YOU'LL FIND OUT. YOU'LL SEE WHEN KING WILLIAM ENTERS THE SCENE...

THERE'S NO WAY.

YOU WON'T HURT ANYONE WITH THAT SWORD.

WHAT'S WITH THE HAT?

I'M NOT A WITCH LIKE YOU, MONICA...

THAT WE CAN BE GOOD MONARCHS.

WE WILL.

IT'S A SYMBOL.

IT MEANS THAT WE'RE NOT DIFFERENT FROM THEM.

NOT ANYMORE.

WE'LL FIGHT TO GET DANI BACK, BUT ALSO TO ACHIEVE PEACE.

IT MEANS THAT WE'RE NOT OUR FATHERS.

NOT SO FAST!

HAH! WHAT A BLOW!

CAREFUL, YOU IDIOT!

DON'T HURT THE QUEEN!

WHAT WERE YOU GONNA DO TO HER?

LOCK HER UP IN A DUNGEON, JUST LIKE MRS. WYTTE?

YOU'RE WRONG. DANI IS MY FRIEND.

THE QUEEN OF WITCHES WOULDN'T BE FRIENDS WITH SOMEONE LIKE YOU.

SOMEONE LIKE ME?

FOR YOUR INFORMATION, WE'RE THE SAME. I'M A WITCH TOO.

DON'T HURT ANYONE THOUGH!

WE CAN SOLVE THIS PEACEFULLY.

YOU SEEM VERY CONFIDENT...

TRUST ME, AISHA.

AWESOME!

BRUTAL.

HE GOT PETRIFIED. THAT'S A GOOD ONE.

IT WORKED!

IT'S JUST LIKE CASTING SPELLS.

WE MAKE A GOOD TEAM.

YES. I FEEL POWERFUL!

I COULD TEACH YOU HOW TO SHOOT AN ARROW IF YOU WANT.

THAT'D BE WONDERFUL...!

AH...

MONICA!

NO!

DISENCHANT THE QUEEN.

NOW.

UNDO YOUR SPELL.

WAIT, DORIAN!

DON'T ATTACK HIM!

DORIAN, NO...!

NOT LIKE THIS!

I WON'T ASK TWICE.

ALL RIGHT!

ALL RIGHT, I'M LETTING HER GO!

AH...!

NO!

LEAVE HIM ALONE!

WHY ARE YOU SO CRUEL?

WE ONLY WANTED OUR QUEEN!

WE DON'T WANT TO GO BACK TO HOW IT WAS BEFORE...

BECAUSE OF HER...

WE COULD WALK THE STREETS WITHOUT ANY FEAR FOR THE FIRST TIME.

THANKS TO HER, WE STOPPED HIDING WHO WE ARE.

DANI...

YOU'RE SO SELFISH.

DANI, I...

I'VE FORGOTTEN SOMETHING IMPORTANT, HAVEN'T I?

WHAT IF WE COULD CHANGE IT?

WHAT IF WE COULD FIX IT ALL WITH OUR WILLPOWER?

WHAT WOULD YOU THINK OF ME NOW?

'CAUSE YOU NEVER DID ANYTHING WRONG.

NEVER.

I FEEL LIKE I'VE DISAPPOINTED YOU.

FOR JUST A SECOND, I'D LIKE TO STOP FEELING ANYTHING, ONCE AND FOR ALL.

ONCE AGAIN.

I THINK NICO...

...IS DYING.

WHA...?

BA-DUMP

EMOTIONLESS...

COMPLETELY EMOTIONLESS...

SHE...

SHE MUST HAVE SUFFERED A GREAT DEAL WHEN SHE SAW YOU DIE, DORIAN...

AND SHE WANTED TO ERASE THAT PAIN.

ERASING EVERYTHING ELSE ALONG WITH IT.

"THERE'S SOMETHING WAY MORE POWERFUL..." THAT MEANS...

THAT MEANS THAT IF DANI LOSES HER MAGICAL POWERS, THE CURSE WILL BE BROKEN?

AH...

MAY...

MAYBE.

DORIAN.

THIS IS THE POTION I USED ON YOUR MOTHER.

BUT...

DANI WOULD
BE BACK...

WITHOUT
HER POWERS,
THOUGH.

PERHAPS THIS
IS WHAT SHE WANTS.
SHE WAS NEVER
ENTIRELY HAPPY WITH
THEM EITHER.

ALTHOUGH...

WHY DOES IT
HURT SO MUCH TO
THINK OF IT?

WHAT
ELSE CAN
WE DO?

DANI...

... ALL RIGHT.

COUGH

COUGH

COUGH

NICO!

WE NEED TO
FIND SOMEONE
WHO'S ABLE TO
HEAL HIM.

THERE ARE
MANY WITCHES,
MAYBE SOMEONE
CAN HELP.

NICO?
ARE YOU THERE?
SPEAK TO ME, SAY
SOMETHING...

TELL MARK I
CAN SMELL HIS
ARMPITS...

THE VILLAGE IS
A WRECK...

329

THEY HAVEN'T STOPPED FIGHTING... WITCHES AGAINST WITCHES.

THIS DOESN'T MAKE ANY SENSE.

WHAT ARE WE GONNA DO?

I DON'T KNOW...

THAT'S ENOUGH!

EVERYBODY.

STOP.

CAN'T YOU SEE WHAT YOU'RE DOING?!

YOU FIGHT FOR THE FREEDOM OF WITCHES...

BY ATTACKING OTHER WITCHES?!

IT'S OVER.

IT'S NOT OVER.

WE WANT OUR QUEEN.

330

LET'S MAKE A DEAL.

WE HEAL YOUR FRIEND.

YOU GIVE US OUR QUEEN AND ALLOW US TO LEAVE.

WE WON'T BOTHER YOU ANYMORE. WE'LL LEAVE AND LIVE OUR LIFE FAR AWAY.

WHERE NOBODY WILL LOCK US UP OR BURN US.

WE NEED THE QUEEN, THOUGH.

SHE'S OUR SYMBOL, THE LIGHT OF A TORCH THAT'LL GUIDE WHOEVER IS LOOKING FOR A BETTER PLACE.

WE WON'T ALLOW YOU TO LOCK HER UP.

DANIELA WYTTE IS MY SISTER. WE JUST WANT TO HEAL HER.

331

WE NEED TO
BE BETTER THAN
THAT.

STOP
BLABBERING!

DO YOU THINK I
WEAR THIS 'CAUSE
IT'S COOL?!

WELL, MAYBE
JUST A LITTLE.
IT LOOKS REALLY
CUTE ON ME.

BUT IT'S ALSO MY SYMBOLIC GESTURE TOWARDS YOU.

TOWARDS EVERYONE!

WE AREN'T GONNA LOCK ANYBODY UP!

NOT THOSE WHO DO MAGIC AND NOT YOUR QUEEN.

YOU CAN REST ASSURED.

SORRY IF I CAN'T ACTUALLY TRUST YOU...

YOUR FRIEND IS WOUNDED.

MINE TOO.

WE'RE ALL IN THE SAME BOAT.

THIS CLEARLY GOT A BIT OUT OF HAND.

BUT I KNOW THAT NEITHER SIDE WAS AIMING TO KILL.

I'M ONLY ASKING FOR YOUR HELP.

I'VE SEEN YOU AIM AT OTHER PLACES, AT THE WALLS, TRYING TO INTIMIDATE US, BUT WITHOUT HURTING US.

PLEASE, WE CAN FIX THIS.

...

WELL...

MARTHA?

MARTHA!

WHAT ARE YOU DOING?

YOU'RE THE KING, AREN'T YOU?

DO YOU AGREE WITH EVERYTHING YOUR WIFE SAID?

DO YOU ALSO PROMISE YOU'RE GOING TO ENSURE THE SAFETY OF ALL WITCHES?

PROMISE ME NOBODY IN MY GROUP WILL END UP IN THE DUNGEONS.

WELL...

ALMOST NOBODY.

OF COURSE.

I SWEAR.

UH...

THANK YOU SO MUCH.

AND HOW MANY HAVE BECOME INTERESTED IN MAGIC OVER THE LAST COUPLE OF YEARS?

AND WHAT DOES IT MATTER, WHO STARTED FIRST AND WHO CAME LATER?

WE WERE ALL...

IDIOTS.

WE WERE ALL IDIOTS.

WE CAN CREATE SOMETHING NEW, THOUGH, ALL TOGETHER.

SOMETHING STRONGER AND BETTER.

WE'LL START BY RECONSTRUCTING THE VILLAGE,

JUST LIKE WE DID WITH THE MASTER'S HOUSE.

OH, THAT'S A GOOD IDEA!

MY HOUSE WAS TOTALLY SHATTERED!

WILL IT BE FREE?

THE FAÇADE OF MY HOUSE COULD REALLY USE A COAT OF PAINT.

IF YOU WANDER OFF, THE CYCLE WILL START AGAIN.

YOU DON'T NEED TO FEAR THE FUTURE.

I WAS ALSO SCARED.

BUT FEAR ISN'T FOREVER.

STAY HERE. SHARE. MIX. COEXIST.

AND THEN PAST FEAR WON'T COME BACK.

NOT IF WE ALL STICK TOGETHER.

IT DOESN'T HAVE TO BE ALL BLACK AND GLOOMY.

HA-HA!

OH?

MY LATE FATHER-IN-LAW FORBADE PUNISHING WITCHES FOR DOING MAGIC.

IT WAS MANY YEARS AGO,

ALTHOUGH SOME PEOPLE LIKE MY FATHER DIDN'T RESPECT THAT RULE.

MONICA AND I, AS THE NEW QUEEN AND KING, ARE GOING TO TAKE A STEP FORWARD.

I DID ALL I COULD...

NOW HE NEEDS TO REST...

THANK YOU SO MUCH, REALLY.

AH...

OH... HOW LOVELY...

STARTING FROM NOW,

MAGIC WILL BE FOR EVERYONE.

DAMIEN...

I CAN SEE YOU MELTING.

!

SHUT UP!

HA-HA!

A WORLD IN WHICH MAGIC WILL BE FOR EVERYONE...

SOUNDS GOOD...

FOR EVERYONE EXCEPT FOR...

DORIAN!

DID YOU DO THIS?!

DORIAN...?

MMM?

IS IT REALLY YOU?

OF COURSE IT'S ME.

DANI?

BUT... I THINK I SAW YOU DIE...

YOU GOT BURNED.

I...

WAS IT A DREAM?

DID I MAKE IT ALL UP?

NO, YOU DIDN'T MAKE IT UP.

IT HAPPENED, BUT THAT WASN'T ME.

THIS IS REAL.

DANIII!

AH!

WE'VE MISSED YOU!

I'M SO GLAD YOU'RE BACK!

AW, I LOVE YOUR SMILE! YOU LOOK SO DIFFERENT NOW!

DAMIEN.

GO GIVE OUR SISTER A HUG.

COME ON.

NO.

HUUUH?

WHY NOT?!

COME ON, DON'T BE SHY!

I SAID NO! SHE'LL THINK I'M WEIRD!

I'M GLAD YOU'RE OK!

THANK YOU, ANNE!

WAS I NOT DOING WELL?

ARGH!

DANI!

ARE YOU OK?

YES, I JUST TRIPPED OVER...

...MY HAIR?

WHAT...?

THIS HAIR IS STUPIDLY LONG.

AH! AND WHAT ABOUT THIS DRESS?!

I LOOK OLD!

NOW THAT YOU'RE NOT AN EVIL OVERLADY ANYMORE, IT DOESN'T SUIT YOU, TO BE HONEST.

SO YOU HAVE NO MEMORY AT ALL OF THE LAST THREE YEARS?

AH, HI DAMIEN.

I THINK...

...I DO?

I'M NOT SURE. I FEEL DIZZY...

AH...

WAIT.

NICO!

WELL, HE'S STILL UNCONSCIOUS.

HE HAS STOPPED BLEEDING THOUGH.

AH... MAJESTY.

WAIT.

DANI JUST WENT THROUGH A MAJOR SHOCK.

SHE NEEDS
TO REST.

WE ALL
DO.

LET'S TAKE
SOME TIME TO REGAIN
OUR STRENGTH.

WE WILL
MEET LATER.

MY HUSBAND
AND I HAVE AN OFFER
FOR YOU.

THOSE WITCHES
RECONSTRUCTED THE
ROOFTOP IN JUST A
FEW MINUTES.

AMAZING!

WITH THEIR HELP
WE WILL FINISH IN
NO TIME!

WE NEED
MORE STONE.
THESE FACADES ARE
TOTALLY WRECKED.

WILL THERE
BE ENOUGH
MONEY?

KING WILLIAM
SAID HE'LL TAKE
CARE OF THE
EXPENSES.

IT TURNS OUT
HE'S A GOOD GUY
AFTER ALL.

HE HAS SOME
GUTS, THAT'S
FOR SURE!

353

HEY...

UH...

A... ARE YOU OK?

NICO...?

IS THIS REALLY YOU?

IT'S NOT A DREAM, IS IT?

AH?

NO!

IT'S ME!

I WANTED TO THANK YOU...

HANG ON.

JUST A SECOND.

I NEED TO PROCESS IT.

I CAN'T BELIEVE I'M TALKING TO YOU...

AND THAT YOU'RE ANSWERING BACK...

I'M SORRY FOR NOT ANSWERING UNTIL NOW.

I WANTED TO THANK YOU FOR BEING BY MY SIDE, NICO.

FOR NOT LEAVING ME ALONE EVEN THOUGH...

MAYBE I DESERVED IT.

YOU WEREN'T DOING WELL.

I WASN'T GOING TO ABANDON YOU BECAUSE OF THAT.

YOU REMEMBER EVERYTHING, THEN?

WELL...

IT'S WEIRD, A BIT LIKE A DREAM.

GLIMPSES OF FOGGY MEMORIES ARE COMING TO ME, MORE AND MORE.

...

WHAT?

I'M SORRY.

I'M JUST REALLY NERVOUS. I STILL CAN'T BELIEVE IT.

NICO...

HOW WAS THE CURSE BROKEN?

IT HAPPENED WHEN WILLIAM AND MONICA WERE TALKING TO THE PEOPLE.

THEY WERE PROMISING THEM A BETTER FUTURE.

DORIAN MADE A LOT OF COLORFUL HATS FLY,

IT WAS BEAUTIFUL...

AND SUDDENLY I FELT AS IF...

AS IF I HAD BEEN LOCKED INSIDE A SMALL ROOM,

DARK AND DUSTY,

AND THEN A DOOR OPENED,

BATHING EVERYTHING WITH LIGHT.

IT WAS LIKE...

...GETTING OUT OF A PRISON CELL.

I FIGURED IT...

IT WASN'T JUST DORIAN'S "DEATH", WAS IT?

WHAT HURT YOU, WHAT MADE YOU WANT TO DISAPPEAR.

IT WAS ALSO ALEX, YOUR DAD,

ALL THE TIMES YOU'VE FELT TRAPPED BETWEEN TWO SIDES IN A TERRIBLE CONFLICT.

YES, YOU'RE RIGHT.

NICO, YOU GOT SO SMART.

I'M NOT SMART.

THIS IS ALL I COULD COME UP WITH IN THREE YEARS.

AND EVEN THEN, IT TOOK ME A WHILE TO REALIZE IT.

NICOOO! YOU'VE SCARED US A LOT!

HEY!

I'M SORRY!

HOW ARE YOU FEELING?

PERFECTLY WELL!

DID YOU SEE?

YES, SHE'S BACK WITH US.

OUCH!

WHAT ON EARTH ARE YOU WEARING, DANI?

AH! I BORROWED IT FROM MARK.

AH! HE BEAT ME TO IT!

MARK, WAIT 'TIL I CATCH YOU...

OF COURSE, MUFFIN BOY.

REGARDLESS, I CAN'T ALLOW YOU TO WEAR THAT.

LUCKILY, YOUR DEAR MONICA IS HERE!

COME, COME, LET'S TRY SOME DRESSES ON.

AH, WAIT...!

NICO, I'M JUST TAKING HER FOR A WHILE.

YOU EXPERIENCED TOO MANY STRONG EMOTIONS IN A SINGLE DAY, AND YOU'RE WOUNDED.

LET YOUR HEART REST FOR A BIT.

...

OHHH, DANI, I'M SO GLAD YOU'RE HERE!

SERIOUSLY?

CONSIDER IT DONE!

HEY, DANI.

ARE YOU READY?

DORIAN...!

HEY, WE'RE MATCHING!

I KNOW!

IT COULDN'T BE ANY OTHER WAY.

WE WILL MAKE AN IMPECCABLE IMPRESSION ON THE PEOPLE.

HOW ARE YOU FEELING? NERVOUS?

I NEED TO CONVINCE ALL THOSE PEOPLE NOT TO KILL MONICA, AND THEREUPON ABDICATE IN HER FAVOR.

INCREDIBLY.

DON'T WORRY.

IF I SEE YOU STRUGGLE, I'LL BE THERE TO CHANGE A FEW HAT COLORS HERE AND THERE!

THANK YOU SO MUCH, DORIAN!

JUST THINK THAT AFTER THIS, YOU WON'T BE THE QUEEN ANYMORE.

YOU WILL BE FREE TO MAKE YOUR OWN DECISIONS.

361

MY DECISIONS...?

HOW ABOUT YOU, DORIAN?

DANI, HURRY UP,

YOU NEED TO GO OUT AT THE SAME TIME AS MONICA!

HAVE YOU DECIDED WHAT YOU WANT TO DO?

YES, I'VE MADE UP MY MIND.

COME ON, DANI. THEY'RE WAITING FOR YOU.

GET READY AS WELL, DORIAN.

...

THANK YOU ALL SO MUCH FOR COMING HERE TODAY.

WE HAVE A BIG ANNOUNCEMENT TO MAKE.

SOMETHING THAT WILL CHANGE THE WORLD FOREVER.

RUN, JULIA!

WE'RE GONNA MISS THE BUS!

JUST DON'T RUN SO FAST!

OH NO, IT'S LEAVING ALREADY!

I CAN ONLY COME UP WITH ONE THING.

WAAAIT!

HURRY UP, GET ON THE BROOM.

WAIT, KIDS...

THAT'S DANGEROUS...

OH!

WHOA!

AWESOME!

SCREEECH

HEY, YOU! WHAT DO YOU THINK YOU'RE DOING?

THAT WAS DANGEROUS!

WE COULDN'T MISS THE FIRST DAY OF CLASS!

THANK YOU FOR STOPPING!

THANKS!

YEAH, BUT YOU DIDN'T NEED TO GO SO FAST ON THAT BROOM...

IT'S NOT LIKE THE SCHOOL IS HIDDEN.

GOOD MORNING, EVERYONE.

AS YOU KNOW, THIS COURSE IS PART OF A GREAT EDUCATIONAL REFORM.

HOW HANDSOME...

I HOPE HE'S GONNA BE OUR NEW TUTOR...

STARTING NOW, A NUMBER OF SUBJECTS WILL BE ADDED,

INCLUDING POTION-MAKING, FLYING ON A BROOM,

ELEMENTAL SPELLS, DOMESTIC SPELLS, DIVINATION, AND SO FORTH...

DORIAAAN!

SORRY FOR BEING SO LATE!

HOW WAS YOUR DAY?

YES... I WANTED TO PROPERLY REVIEW TOMORROW'S CLASS.

AH. WHAT ARE YOU UP TO? STILL READING?

IT'LL BE CRUCIAL, YOU KNOW?

WE'RE GONNA GIVE STUDENTS THEIR FIRST TEST.

YOU'VE WORKED ENOUGH FOR TODAY.

OH!

CAKE?!

HE HE, TONIGHT WE'LL HAVE CAKE FOR DINNER.

MARK GAVE IT TO ME, FOR YOU.

WE SHOULD EAT CAKE EVERY DAY.

AND NOW, WE'LL LEAVE YOU TO SOME MUSICAL MOMENTS.

DORIAN...

I SAW DAMIEN TODAY.

HOW DID IT GO? DID YOU TALK?

HE ASKED ME...

IF WE'RE READY TO GO AND SEE MUM.

...

... YES.

WE SHOULD GO.

DAMIEN!

GOOD MORNING.

YOU'RE LATE.

SORRY TO KEEP YOU WAITING.

WOW! WHAT'S WITH THE OUTFIT?

DID YOU DRESS UP LIKE THAT FOR MUM?

SHUT UP.

...

WHAT HAPPENED WITH THE PRISONERS OF WAR, DAMIEN?

AS FOR THE OTHERS, WELL...

THOSE WHO DID NOT COMMIT VIOLENT CRIMES WON'T RECEIVE ANY CHARGES.

MOST OF THEM HAVE BEEN DEPORTED AND DEPRIVED OF THEIR MAGICAL POWERS.

AUNT HILDE SAID THAT SHE DIDN'T CARE IF SHE LOST HER MAGIC,

BUT STILL, SINCE SHE WAS ONE OF THE LEADERS, SHE HAD TO PAY A LARGE SUM OF MONEY AS COMPENSATION.

THOSE FUNDS WILL GO DIRECTLY TO THE SCHOOL.

AUNT HILDE...

AND WHERE IS SHE NOW?

POOR THING, SHE REALLY LOVED HER MONEY.

I HEARD THAT SHE SET UP A POTION BUSINESS IN THE OUTSKIRTS OF THE KINGDOM.

IT'S GOING PRETTY WELL.

UM...

WHAT ABOUT THE MASTER? IS HE STILL IN JAIL?

PENDRAGON...

HE WAS BROKE, BUT HE WAS DEPRIVED OF HIS POWERS AND DEPORTED.

HE LEFT SILENTLY, WITH HIS HEAD LOW.

WE HAVEN'T HEARD ABOUT HIM EVER SINCE.

I DON'T THINK...

WE'LL EVER SEE HIM AGAIN.

AND THEN THERE'S HER,

ANGELA WYTTE.

MUM.

HELLO, MUM.

GOOD MORNING!

YOU'RE A BIT LATE TODAY!

DAMIEN!

I KNOW, I'M SORRY.

I HAD SOMETHING TO DO.

HAVE YOU ALREADY HAD BREAKFAST, SWEETHEART?

NO, OF COURSE NOT.

WE'RE GONNA HAVE BREAKFAST TOGETHER AS ALWAYS, RIGHT?

AH...

...

HI, MUM.

OH, WELL, I HAVE ALREADY EATEN! I'M SORRY!

OH, COME ON...!

DORIAN...

DANI...

YOU CAME...

MUM!

I'M GLAD TO SEE YOU'RE FINE.

DANI, SWEETHEART...

WHAT HAPPENED?

I DON'T KNOW.

BUT EVERYTHING'S OKAY NOW.

...

MUM, DANI AND I ARE LIVING TOGETHER CLOSE BY.

I THOUGHT YOU COULD ALSO SETTLE...

DORIAN.

MUM IS GONNA LIVE HERE WITH ME, AT THE PALACE.

SHE'LL BE FINE. THERE'S NOTHING TO WORRY ABOUT.

SHE WON'T BE LOCKED UP.

IT'S NOT A PROBLEM FOR ME AT ALL.

SHE'S MY MOTHER.

AND ALSO MINE.

I'VE ALLOWED YOU TO TAKE ALL THE RESPONSIBILITY FOR WAY TOO LONG.

YOU NEED TO GET ON WITH YOUR LIVES. YOU'RE STILL KIDS.

LET ME DO THIS.

MOREOVER, I LIKE HAVING HER HERE.

COME ON,

GIVE HER A HUG.

SHE SAYS SHE HAS NOWHERE TO GO,

BECAUSE IT DOESN'T MAKE SENSE TO BE SEPARATED FROM HER KIDS.

PERHAPS, LITTLE BY LITTLE, OVER TIME...

WE'LL MANAGE TO BE A FAMILY AGAIN.

I'M OFF TO SCHOOL, DANI.

WHAT ARE YOU UP TO TODAY?

AH? WELL, I SUPPOSE...

NOTHING.

I'LL CRASH ON THE SOFA.

COME ON, DON'T SAY THAT.

WHEN I'M BACK, WE COULD GO FOR A NOCTURNAL PICNIC.

BYE!

...

SOUNDS GOOD...

BUT...

...

BUT I CAN'T GO ON LIKE THIS.

DORIAN, MONICA, DAMIEN, WILLIAM, MARK, EVEN NICO...

EVERYONE ELSE IS MAKING DECISIONS, LIVING THEIR LIVES, AND DOING GREAT AND KIND THINGS.

WHAT CAN I DO, THOUGH?

I NEED TO STOP BEING LAZY AND MAKE UP MY MIND!

I GOT IT! ONLY ONE PLACE CAN HELP ME FIGURE OUT MY FUTURE!

THAT'S ALL FOR TODAY!

SEE YOU TOMORROW, PROFESSOR WYTTE!

HI, PROFESSOR WYTTE!

ARE YOU FREE TO GO ON A DATE WITH ME YET?

MONICA!

WHAT ARE YOU DOING HERE?!

IF THE CHILDREN DISCOVER US, IT WILL BE A DISASTER!

SO YOU'RE ENJOYING YOUR LIFE AS A TEACHER?

I LOVE IT!

SEEING THE CHILDREN'S PROGRESS IN MAGIC IS WONDERFUL.

AND I SPEND MOST OF MY TIME READING!

I'M BUILDING MY DREAM LIBRARY AT HOME!

I'LL BORROW YOUR FAVORITE NOVELS, THEN!

I DON'T HAVE ANY...

I THINK NOVELS ARE A WASTE OF TIME. YOU CAN'T LEARN ANYTHING FROM THEM.

ARE YOU KIDDING?!

READ SOME OF THEM, YOU WON'T REGRET IT!

THEY'VE INSPIRED ME AND MADE ME GROW!

I'LL READ THEM ALL.

IN NOVELS YOU CAN LEARN ABOUT LIFE, ABOUT THE VERY ESSENCE OF HUMAN BEINGS!

WHAT?!

I LOVE HOW PASSIONATE YOU ARE ABOUT IT.

I WANT US TO EXPERIENCE TOGETHER THE THINGS THAT MAKE YOU HAPPY!

DORIAN...

AH!

I'M EXPERIENCING A SECRET, FORBIDDEN LOVE STORY.

HOW EXCITING!

DO YOU THINK I'M THE WORST FOR ENJOYING THIS SO MUCH?

I THINK YOU READ TOO MANY NOVELS.

HA-HA!

HELLO, CAN I COME IN?

YES, COME ON IN...

WHAT DO YOU WANNA KN...?

THE ALLEY OF THE FUTURE

CLAIRVOYANTS AND FORTUNE-TELLERS FOR ALL BUDGETS.

AH.

IT'S YOU, DANI!

I'LL NEED TO USE MY POWERS FOR REAL NOW.

DON'T YOU DO THAT FOR YOUR CLIENTS?!

WHY WOULD I? I DRAW THE CARDS, MAKE UP SOMETHING FOOLISH, AND GET THE CASH.

ZERO COMPLICATIONS.

YOU WOULDN'T BELIEVE HOW GOOD I AM AT IMPROVISING!

WOW, HOW COOL!

I WANT YOU TO GIVE ME A READING!

ALL RIGHT, SO, WHAT'S YOUR QUESTION?

WHAT'S ON YOUR MIND?

377

378

DO YOU ALREADY KNOW EVERYTHING BY HEART, DANI?

YES!

WELL, MORE OR LESS.

I'LL STUDY ON THE WAY. I PROMISE!

JUST IN CASE YOU FORGET SOMETHING, YOU'VE GOT MY SIGNED REPORTS.

ALTHOUGH, ANYONE WOULD WANT TO STUDY MAGIC JUST BY LOOKING AT THAT ADORABLE OUTFIT.

YOU'RE THE BEST MESSENGER I COULD WISH FOR!

AND YOU DIDN'T ORDER A UNIFORM FOR NICO, MONICA?

I WANTED TO SEE IT.

I WON'T BE WORKING AS A MESSENGER!

I'M ONLY GOING WITH DANI TO EARN SOME CASH FROM UNWISE NEW CLIENTS.

YEAH, I'M SURE THAT'S THE MAIN REASON WHY YOU'RE GOING WITH HER...

AH! HELLO WILLIAM. HI DAMIEN!

SEE? SHE HASN'T LEFT YET!

I TOLD YOU!

DAMIEN WAS AFRAID YOU LEFT BEFORE HE COULD SAY GOODBYE, DANI.

HUH?

REALLY?

DON'T WORRY, I'M ONLY GONNA BE GONE FOR A FEW WEEKS!

YEAH, BUT IT'S YOUR FIRST TRIP ON YOUR OWN AS A MESSENGER...

I THOUGHT I COULD GIVE YOU SOME ADVICE, PERHAPS... AS YOUR OLDER BROTHER...

I'M NOT GOING ON MY OWN!

NICO IS COMING WITH ME.

HEY!

...

THEN I'M GONNA GIVE A PIECE OF ADVICE TO YOU INSTEAD...

HEY, YOU'RE FREAKING ME OUT!

385

YES,
I'M SURE
OF IT.

I WILL
KEEP ON DOING
MY BEST.

WE ALL
WILL.

WE WILL WORK
TOGETHER

WITH WHAT WE
HAVE, WITH EVERYTHING
WE HAVE LEARNED.

SO THAT, LITTLE
BY LITTLE,

WE WILL BE
ABLE TO RECTIFY
PAST MISTAKES,

AND CREATE A
BETTER WORLD FOR
EVERYONE.

THE END

•EPILOGUE•

TELL ME, MY DEAR CHILDREN...

HOW ARE YOUR LOVE LIVES GOING?

COME ON, DON'T BE SHY!

TELL YOUR MOM ABOUT YOUR BOYFRIENDS AND GIRLFRIENDS!

I'M SINGLE.

OF COURSE, YOU'RE STILL VERY YOUNG, DANI.

AND SO IS DORIAN.

BUT MY DAMIEN HAS ALREADY REACHED MARRIAGEABLE AGE.

TELL ME, SWEETHEART, IS THERE A GIRL WHO HAS STOLEN YOUR HEART?

HOW AM I SUPPOSED TO TELL HER?

NO, THERE'S NO GIRL...

PERFECT, BECAUSE I'VE BEEN THINKING...

SINCE WE'RE NOW FOLLOWING THIS "PEACEFUL" ROUTE AND YOU THREE HAVE CONNECTIONS TO ROYALTY...

YOU, DAMIEN, COULD SEDUCE MONICA.

THEN DANI COULD SEDUCE KING WILLIAM...

...AND WE, THE WYTTES, WILL GET ALL THE POWER OF THE CROWN.

IT'S AN EXCELLENT PLAN...

OH, IT'S FUNNY YOU SHOULD MENTION THAT, MOM...

ACTUALLY, WE HAVE A SLIGHTLY DIFFERENT SUGGESTION.

FARMERS KEEP COMPLAINING THAT SOME FIELDS ARE STILL BARREN BECAUSE OF THE MAGIC WARS.

AHA...

I SUGGEST THAT MONICA SET UP RESEARCH IN HER POTIONS LAB TO FIND SOMETHING THAT CAN RETURN FERTILITY TO THE LAND.

SOUNDS GOOD.

HOWEVER, THERE IS SOMETHING IMPORTANT I WOULD LIKE TO CONSULT YOU ON, DAMIEN...

WHAT?

I WOULD LIKE TO REWARD YOUR LOYALTY AS A ROYAL ADVISER BY TAKING YOU TO DINNER.

WHAT DO YOU SAY?

WILL!

I MEAN...YOUR MAJESTY!

OF COURSE I ACCEPT YOUR HONORABLE REWARD.

DO THOSE TWO EVEN TRY TO HIDE ANYTHING ANYMORE?

POOR QUEEN MONICA, WHAT A HUSBAND...

I HEARD THAT SHE ALSO HAS A WITCH BOY AS A VERY GOOD FRIEND.

393

AH, THERE YOU ARE!

MONICA TOLD ME YOU WANTED TO SEE ME!

HA HA HA

YES... I NEED TO TALK TO YOU...

WHAT ARE YOU DOING WITH YOUR SHIRT ALL BUTTONED UP?

I DON'T KNOW, MONICA SAID IT LOOKS BETTER LIKE THIS.

TO CONQUER A GIRL'S HEART, YOU HAVE TO BE CLASSY AND CHIVALROUS!

BUTTON UP YOUR SHIRT, NICO!

AND GOOD LUCK!

MONICA HAS NO IDEA!

IT DOESN'T SUIT YOU.

AH!

WELL, THIS IS IT!

THANK YOU SO MUCH FOR READING THIS FAR. I HOPE YOU ENJOYED READING *HOOKY* AS MUCH AS I ENJOYED WRITING IT.

I STARTED CREATING THIS STORY ALMOST BY CHANCE IN 2015, AS MANY OF YOU KNOW, ON THE WEBTOON PLATFORM.

AND IN EARLY 2020 I FINISHED DRAWING THE ADVENTURES OF DANI AND DORIAN. AT THE TIME I'D ALREADY SAID GOODBYE TO THEM (AND TO THE READERS!), AND I DIDN'T THINK THAT THREE YEARS LATER I WOULD BE SAYING GOODBYE TO THEM AGAIN AND PROBABLY FOR GOOD.

THE TRUTH IS THAT I STILL FIND IT HARD TO BELIEVE!

HOOKY HAS BEEN WITH ME FOR EIGHT YEARS OF MY LIFE! IT HAS MEANT A LOT OF WORK AND DEDICATION. FIRST, IN WEBTOON, I WROTE AND DREW ONE EPISODE PER WEEK. THE TRUTH IS THAT THE DEADLINES SOMETIMES WERE A STRUGGLE FOR ME. THEN, I HAD TO TRANSLATE THE WHOLE STORY INTO THE LANGUAGE OF TRADITIONAL COMICS. THIS MEANT DOING A REVISION AND REORGANIZATION OF ABSOLUTELY EVERYTHING.

BUT IT WAS WORTH EVERY MINUTE OF IT. TO BE ABLE TO SHARE MY STORIES WITH THE WORLD AND SEE THAT ON THE OTHER SIDE, OTHERS ENJOY THEM WITH THE SAME INTENSITY AS I DO, IS SOMETHING ABSOLUTELY WONDERFUL.

THANK YOU SO MUCH FOR YOUR SUPPORT. TRULY.

FOR EVERY COMMENT ON WEBTOON AND ON MY SOCIAL MEDIA, FOR EVERY VIDEO EDIT, FOR EVERY FANART, FOR EVERY TIME YOU CAME TO THE SIGNINGS AND TOLD ME HOW MUCH YOU LIKED THE STORY, OR HOW MUCH YOU LOVED THIS OR THAT CHARACTER. I'M DELIGHTED WHEN YOU TELL ME THAT MY STORY HAS ENCOURAGED YOU TO CREATE YOUR OWN, OR WHEN YOU CONFESS THAT MY COMIC WAS THE ONE THAT MADE YOU FALL IN LOVE WITH READING.

YOU ALL MAKE IT ALL MAKE SENSE.

DANI, DORIAN, AND THE WHOLE GANG WILL ALWAYS HAVE A VERY SPECIAL PLACE IN MY HEART. THEY ARE MY KIDS! I'VE GROWN UP WITH THEM, BOTH AS A PERSON AND AS AN ARTIST. BUT NOW IT'S TIME TO SAY GOODBYE. I'M GOING TO MISS THEM A LOT.

(ALTHOUGH, TO BE HONEST, I DON'T THINK I'LL BE ABLE TO AVOID DRAWING THEM FROM TIME TO TIME!)

THANKS FOR EVERYTHING,

MÍRIAM BONASTRE TUR
2023